Hooked

Kate Davies

Kate Davies Romance

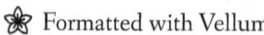

To John and Lori. Thanks for taking the time to read this manuscript and help out with the fishing details. It's greatly appreciated! (Any errors, of course, are my own.) I'm so proud to call you family.

Chapter One

W ell, there was no doubt about it.
    Madison McIntyre had been banished to the
    ends of the earth.

She pulled into a parking space on the main street of Westport and killed the engine. She probably should be on her way to The Inn, get settled in before it was too dark, but she desperately needed time to regroup.

Her trunk was filled with two suitcases, a briefcase, and her laptop. She'd barely had time to pack after receiving this assignment, and knew just by looking down the street that she was going to stick out here like a prom dress on a linebacker.

To her left was a three-block strip of shops hawking kites, fish and chips, and t-shirts adorned with imitation seagull droppings. A few stragglers peered in windows, but most of the stores were closed up tight and the sidewalk was nearly deserted. To her right was the waterfront.

Row after row of boats crowded the docks, trim sailboats rubbing elbows with crusty old fishing vessels. The sharp tang of salt permeated the early-evening breeze. Madison rolled up the window, silently cursing the effect the maritime wind would have on her hair. She probably needed to resign herself to tangled, frizzy locks for the next month.

A month! Madison sighed, resting her forehead against the steering wheel for a moment. She was stuck here for the next four weeks, and if she didn't get the job done, there wouldn't *be* a job to return to in Seattle.

And without a job, there wasn't much of a reason to return at all.

Acid churned in her gut at the thought. Granted, her position at Donovan Development wasn't anything to shout about, but just the idea of losing her job made her queasy. She needed the security, the stability, the retirement plan and health insurance. She needed her tidy little cubicle with its office-friendly plants and tasteful framed photos. Anything outside that comfort zone scared her half to death.

Which was probably why her smarmy boss had shoved her out the door so quickly on this assignment.

Madison mentally shook herself. So what if three other Donovan executives had tried—and failed—to get the Westport project off the ground. So what if they had all subsequently "resigned". She would be successful even if it killed her.

The scent of raw fish seeped into the interior of her car and she groaned. A month in this town could very well do her in.

"Welcome to The Inn." The rosy-cheeked, Mrs. Claus-lookalike at the front desk handed Madison the key to her cabin. "What brings you to Westport?"

"Actually, I'm—on sabbatical," Madison said, a weak smile tilting the corners of her mouth briefly. She didn't normally make a habit of lying, but the horror stories about the "Westport Curse", bandied about the staff room in muted whispers, had convinced her she had to be extra cautious about proclaiming her intentions.

The first Donovan Development employee to bring their resort plans to town had been unceremoniously escorted to the city limits and told not to return.

As had employees number two and three.

Donovan Development was not a popular company in Westport.

"How nice." Ronnie Edwards's white bun bobbed precariously on top of her head as she nodded. "Are you looking for some peace and quiet, or do you want to try out the activities available in town?"

Actually, what I'd really like to do is leave, Madison thought. "Probably a little of both," she replied.

"Then I have a treat for you. How would you like to go salmon fishing tomorrow?"

Madison's smile froze just a bit. "Uhm... fishing?"

"On a charter boat. It's the biggest draw in Westport. Most boats are booked way in advance, but I happen to know that Oceanic Charters had a last-minute cancellation. I'll go ahead and book your spot."

Briefly, Madison thought about protesting, but caught herself just in time. Maybe this was the key to her success. Much as she hated the idea of spending her first day in town on a fishing boat, she had to get to know Westport. Maybe this fishing trip would help her to understand the tourist trade on the coast a little better. It was at least worth a shot.

"Thanks," she heard herself say.

"Lovely!" Mrs. Edwards made a notation on the pad in front of her. "Oh, since you'll be leaving before breakfast I'll make sure to pack you some pastries to go."

"Before breakfast?" Madison glanced at the sign directly

over the woman's head. Fancy script announced *Breakfast, 7 to 8:30.* "How early do I have to be there?"

"A quarter to five, dear. Float eight, right across from the charter office. Oh, and wear something waterproof. You'll be out on the ocean, after all."

With a weak smile, Madison walked out the front door and leaned wearily against the wall. Life just kept getting better and better.

"Mom, what's this?"

Ronnie looked up from her desk, reading glasses perched on the end of her nose. "Your client list for tomorrow, dear."

Dylan sighed and rubbed the back of his neck. He counted to ten mentally and tried again. "I know. I was talking about the *addition* to the list."

His mom smiled fondly. "Oh, Madison is a dear girl. You'll love her."

He wisely let that comment pass and attempted to get the conversation back to the original topic. "Mom, my boat's already fully booked for tomorrow. She can't go."

Ronnie waved a hand dismissively. "Of course she can. She hardly weighs a thing. You won't even notice she's there."

Dylan gritted his teeth. "Mom..." he growled, but she cut him off.

"I already talked to Bob Findley. He's willing to postpone his trip if you insist on keeping your numbers down."

"That's not fair to Mr. Findley," Dylan started, but his mom was talking again.

"He's happy to do it. I'll bring him an apple pie tomorrow, since it was my, well, error in the first place." She fixed him with a narrow-eyed glare. "And be nice to Madison. She'll be here for a month and doesn't know a soul. I thought this would be a nice way for her to meet some people and get to know Westport."

Dylan knew from experience that *meet some people* translated into *meet Dylan*, but merely nodded and gathered up the rest of his paperwork. With a hug for his mom, he continued back to his apartment at the rear of the main house. He checked on Carly, fast asleep in her toddler bed, and finally dropped onto the couch in the main room.

The long day had only been compounded by the discovery of his mother's newest matchmaking attempt. Since his divorce two years ago she had been shoving every eligible female she could find in his direction. And her definition of eligible was generous, to say the least.

His mom had to learn to keep her nose out of his personal life. Not that he had much of one, but still. He was busy running a business, as well as serving on town council—not to mention raising a toddler. He didn't have time to date.

He'd be friendly to this Madison person, but that was all. He just hoped she wasn't expecting more. That would make the fishing trip miserable, indeed.

Dylan leaned on the railing of *The Lucky Strike* and drew in a deep breath of salt air. He closed his eyes briefly and savored it.

Some people complained about the smell of the ocean, but to Dylan it was the best scent around. The crisp tang of salt, the freshness in the air—nothing woke him up better than a lungful of sea breeze.

He nodded at John, who was busy alternating between tying leaders and cutting herring for bait. The young man had started working for him while still in high school. Now in his early twenties, he handled the morning chores like an old pro.

Dylan's attention turned back to the dock, where customers were starting to arrive. One by one, the men walked down the float and boarded the charter vessel.

Eager enthusiasm practically vibrated off the small group as they clustered around Dylan, asking questions and swigging coffee out of metal thermoses. Two or three of the men were locals who had fished with Dylan in the past, but the rest were new to the game.

Dylan checked each name off the passenger manifesto until all were accounted for—except one.

He stifled a sigh. Of course Mom's secret weapon was late. He'd known from the moment he saw her name on the list that Madison McIntyre was going to be trouble.

A low whistle broke his concentration and he looked up, following the collective gaze of his passengers. He blinked twice and shook his head.

A willowy blonde was picking her way down the float, focused completely on keeping her balance on the gently swaying dock. She was dressed head to toe in khaki, with a pair of tan hiking boots completing the look. A wide black belt cinched the waist of her safari-style blouse, emphasizing her very feminine curves. Not a practical outfit for fishing, but one that drew a definite—and unexpected—reaction. A yellow rain slicker was folded over one arm, and a familiar brown bag was clutched in the opposite hand. He'd bet anything it was filled with his mother's signature muffins.

Yeah, she was definitely going to be trouble.

Dylan waved to catch her attention and she walked gingerly to the slip. "You must be Madison," he said, holding out a hand to help her into the boat.

She nodded, flashing a tight-lipped smile, then clutched the railing as the wake of a passing boat lifted *The Lucky Strike* in a rolling motion.

"I'm Dylan, the captain, and John is my deckhand. If you'd like to join the rest of the group, I'll get you acquainted with the fishing equipment and the rules of the road, so to speak."

She nodded again and sidled close to the cluster of men, still keeping one hand on the rail.

Dylan sighed inwardly. At this rate, she'd never get her sea legs. He'd have to keep an extra-close eye on her, to make sure she was okay.

He ignored the little voice in the back of his head suggesting that he wanted to keep an eye on her for entirely different reasons.

He was flirting with her.

Not blatantly, of course. Just a little extra eye contact, a smile that promised more. A touch on the shoulder to steady her when the boat lurched down yet another monster wave. Some pseudo-concerned expression meant to weaken her defenses.

Her defenses were already weak enough, thank you very much.

Her face was green and her hair was limp and tangled from the constant barrage of salt spray. The smell of diesel and burnt coffee, combined with the continual roll of the boat, made her stomach heave. She was decked out head to toe in completely inappropriate "outdoorsy" resort wear, so new the creases hadn't even been worked out yet.

She looked ridiculous.

So why in the world was he coming on to her?

She glanced around at all the other customers. Maybe the

fact that she was the only female on the charter-fishing trip had something to do with it.

Great. She was a target by default.

Well, this couldn't go on. She was in town for work, not a roll in the hay. Especially with a devil-may-care fishing captain. Her father's example had taught her well—stay away from playboys.

"Look." She swallowed down her nausea as the boat pitched down another rolling wave. "I appreciate the thought, but you're wasting your time."

"Excuse me?" Slate blue eyes reflected the rich color of the ocean under the cloudy sky. A puzzled frown settled over his features.

She waved a hand vaguely between them, then clutched the slick railing again as the boat struggled its way back up the wave. "I'm sure lots of women are flattered when someone like you hits on them, but I'm not one of them." Madison winced inwardly at the snobbish tone in her voice. Dimly, she wondered when she'd started channeling her mother.

"You thought I was hitting on you?" Amazingly, he looked almost insulted, his shoulders pulling down and back as he straightened.

"Flirting. Whatever." She could feel a deep blush creeping up her neck. "I mean, it's nothing personal. I'm just not interested."

A muscle worked in Dylan's jaw. "I'll keep that in mind."

Madison nodded briefly, grateful that the confrontation was over. She turned to go, only to be stopped by a strong, calloused hand on her elbow. Even through the damp khaki sleeve she could feel heat spread up her arm. An unfamiliar warmth settled in her chest as her heart raced out of control. Startled, she stepped away, tugging her arm from his grasp.

"Was there something else?" Even to her own ears she

sounded horribly snippy, but the embarrassment of the situation combined with her seasickness did away with her usual restraint.

"Just a question."

She nodded, not trusting her nausea to stay under control.

"You said 'someone like you'. What exactly did you mean by that?"

She glanced around. Some of the other members of the party were starting to eavesdrop, if the tilted heads and hushed whispers were any indication. Why in the world had she started this awful conversation?

"I don't know," she mumbled. Madison gestured at Dylan, the boat, the speck of land on the far horizon. "A resort-town person."

"A resort town person?" He echoed her phrase, a note of disbelief in his voice. "What does that mean? Someone with no ambition? A slacker? A beach bum only interested in a casual fling?"

He was putting words in her mouth, but she was too sick to care. She just stood there, mute and miserable.

Dylan waited, narrowed eyes challenging her to respond, but she said nothing. He shook his head, a mix of anger and disgust on his face. Then he turned on his heel and walked away.

She watched him go, arms wrapped around her waist. Then the boat took another rolling, roller-coaster ride down an angry wave. Madison lurched to the rail and, in front of the deckhand, the other passengers, and the man she'd just publicly insulted, lost her breakfast.

She had a feeling this would be one charter trip Westport would never forget.

Chapter Two

"So how was your day?"

Dylan glanced at his mother briefly, then turned his attention back to Carly and her drawings. "Fine," he replied, oohing at the mix of colors on his daughter's latest masterpiece.

"Pwitty?" Carly asked, hopping from foot to foot with pride.

"Very pretty." He bent down to kiss her on the forehead. She grinned and scampered away, clutching her papers to her chest.

Dylan straightened, noticing that his mom was still in wait mode—hands on hips, lips pursed, head cocked to one side. He lifted an eyebrow and mimicked her stance.

"Dylan Edwards, stop playing! How was your day?"

He crossed into the family room and sank down into the leather recliner. His mother followed, perching on the edge of the couch, nearly as keyed up as Carly had been moments before.

Dylan kicked his feet up onto the coffee table. "It was fine.

We caught our limit. Even got in a little early, as I'm sure you noticed."

"And Madison?" No more beating around the bush, evidently.

"Madison—well. I don't think she enjoyed herself."

"Oh, the poor dear. Seasick?"

"Mmm-hmm." *Among other things*, Dylan thought wryly. Things like rude, snobbish, and full of herself. And he'd had enough of that with Karen to last him a lifetime.

"Well, maybe you can make it up to her," his mother continued.

Dylan looked at her sharply. "I'm not taking her out on the boat again."

"Of course not," Ronnie said. "The poor thing would be miserable."

So would I, Dylan thought.

"But dinner is a different story. Why not take her down to that nice little seafood restaurant on the jetty?"

Dylan cut her off before she could start naming their children. "I'm sure dinner is the farthest thing from her mind right now, Mom. And I'm too busy, anyway."

She scoffed at him. "Too busy to eat? I swear, you just look for excuses not to date."

Bingo.

"But I can take a hint," she said. "I won't say another word."

Dylan waited.

"I just don't understand it," she burst out, proving him right. "Madison is a lovely girl, Dylan. You don't know what you're missing." And on that note, she bustled out of the room.

Dylan shook his head. Madison's behavior on the boat had made her personality quite clear. He knew *exactly* what he was missing.

Any minute now, the bed was going to stop rolling. Madison clutched a pillow to her stomach, squeezing her eyes shut and moaning a little. Even on dry land, the sensation of the waves stayed with her.

She vaguely remembered a friend in college laughingly complaining about "bed spins" after a night of drinking, but until now the concept had remained theoretical.

And she hadn't even had any alcohol.

At least the smell of fish was starting to fade. The moment she stumbled in the door of her cabin, she'd stripped off the sodden khakis and dumped them in a plastic bag, stuffing them in the closet until she could get to a Laundromat. A quick shower took care of the salt in her hair, but she didn't dare spend more time than necessary under the shower spray, as the pulsing water reminded her a little too much of her charter trip.

Madison groaned again, curling up into a tight ball in the center of her four-poster bed. She'd certainly made an impression today—just not the one she'd wanted to make.

To most of the people on board the fishing trip, she was just the miserable wretch clinging to the rail for six hours. But the captain of the boat must have come away with a totally different impression.

Madison winced at the memory. Even a monster-sized case of seasickness was no excuse for the way she had treated Dylan.

So what if he had been flirting with her. Big deal. Even flattering, if she was going to be perfectly candid. But she'd shut him down almost automatically.

Probably because he'd reminded her so much of her father. Good looking, charming, and incapable of saying no to whatever risk came his way. Anyone who deliberately put himself on an itty-bitty boat and went out onto the ocean to battle the massive waves on a daily basis was not someone who avoided risk.

She eased one eye open and tested the stability of the room. It appeared to have returned to solid ground, so she slowly pulled herself to a sitting position. The thick pile of pillows provided a comfortable backrest.

Well, at least there was little chance of bumping into Captain Dylan again. Even in a small town, Madison was sure they would be running in very different circles.

He, no doubt, spent most of his time on the boat giving fishing tours. She would be spending hours on research, as well as meeting with the mayor and city council to ease the path for Donovan's planned resort. No, they wouldn't have reason to meet again.

And the little stab of regret in the pit of her stomach at the thought was just the nausea returning.

A rap at the door interrupted her pity fest and she called for whoever it was to enter.

Ronnie Edwards swooped through the door with a pitying smile and an overladen tray. "How are you feeling, dear?"

Of course she would know by now. Madison was fairly sure half of Westport had heard the story of her fishing trip already.

"Better," she said, vaguely surprised that it was true. The physical symptoms were fading with time; only the emotional effects seemed to be hanging around. A heavy dose of guilt and embarrassment had lodged permanently in her gut.

Ronnie Edwards bustled over to the side of the bed and placed the tray on the nightstand. A steaming mug and a plate of toast shared space with a freshly pressed linen napkin and a bunch of wildflowers in a blue glass vase.

"I know you think food is the last thing you want right now," Ronnie said, "but some weak tea and dry toast is the best cure for seasickness. Eat just a little at a time and you'll feel right as rain in no time at all."

Madison smiled and lifted the warm, heavy mug to her lips. It, like everything else in the rented cabin, was decorated in a floral pattern. She took an experimental sip and was gratified to discover that her stomach was not in the mood to rebel anymore. She sipped again, feeling warm for the first time since she'd stepped foot on that horrible boat.

Ronnie sniffed, her nose wrinkling. "Now. Where did you hide your clothes from today?"

Madison felt her cheeks heat. "My clothes?"

"Sweetie, I was married to a fisherman for thirty-seven years. I'd know that scent anywhere. Why don't you hand them over and I'll get them washed up for you."

"Oh, that's not necessary..."

Ronnie cut her off with a wave of her hand. "I do laundry all day long to keep this place running. It's no problem to add a few extra pieces."

Touched by her thoughtfulness, Madison slid off the bed and pulled the laundry bag out of the closet. "I don't know how to thank you," she began.

"Join us for dinner tonight," Ronnie said.

"I'm not sure having you cook for me would be repayment for doing my laundry," Madison demurred.

"Pish!" Ronnie tucked the laundry bag under her arm. "It'll be nice to have someone new at the table. Come by the main house around six." With a smile, she walked out the door.

Madison picked up a slice of toast and began to nibble. She wasn't quite sure how to react to such overt—*niceness*. She hadn't had someone nurse her through an illness since—well, she couldn't even remember. It was comforting, but a bit disconcerting as well.

14

She could tell that the next month was going to be very different indeed.

Dylan scooped up Carly and deposited her wriggling, giggling toddler body into the high chair at the end of the dining room table. Sometime in the past decade the table had made the transition from old to antique, but his mom still insisted on using it daily. And to be honest, Dylan secretly applauded her decision. A family heirloom like that deserved to be used, not just looked at.

Dylan stopped his meandering thoughts with a frown. There was an extra place setting at the table tonight. What was his mother up to now?

The table was usually full in the morning, as the guests of The Inn enjoyed his mother's fabulous breakfasts. But dinner was family time.

He scattered a handful of goldfish crackers on Carly's tray and walked back into the kitchen. His mom was stirring a soup pot and adding a few last-minute seasonings.

"Who's joining us for dinner, Mom?" She ignored him, falling back on her habit of pretending deafness when she didn't want to talk about something. Stifling a sigh, he picked up the salad bowl and walked back into the dining room.

And nearly dropped the salad on the hardwood floor.

Madison McIntyre was crouching down next to Carly's high chair, handing her a goldfish that had evidently taken a dive moments before. So far she hadn't noticed his entrance.

"My name is Madison. What's your name?"

Carly munched on her cracker and yelled, "Cawwy!"

"Well, nice to meet you, um, Cawwy." Madison brushed some cracker crumbs off the front of her soft yellow dress and placed her hands on her knees. She made it about halfway to a standing position before she caught sight of Dylan.

He watched her, unblinking, as her face blanched white and then turned bright red. Her mouth opened and closed like a fish in a bucket. Dylan probably would have found the humor in the situation if he hadn't been so furious with his mother.

"My daughter's name is Carly. I see my mother has invited you to join us tonight."

"You ... you're ..." Dylan could see the embarrassment swimming in Madison's eyes. She reached out a hand to steady herself, placing it on the back of the nearest chair.

Snob or no snob, she was his mother's guest—and a paying customer of The Inn. Dylan set down the salad and strode around the table to where Madison stood. With barely-concealed annoyance, Dylan reached around her and pulled out the chair, indicating that she should sit.

"I didn't know that you and Mrs. Edwards were related." She picked at her napkin, nervous energy radiating from her like heat from a sunburn.

Her comment stopped him cold for a moment. In most cases, his mom took every opportunity to sing his praises to the chick *du jour*. Even this morning he had assumed Madison knew he was Ronnie's son. Dylan narrowed his eyes, trying to figure out his mother's angle this time.

A flying fish disturbed his reverie as Carly tossed a handful of crackers in his direction. "Food!" she crowed, banging a chubby fist on the tray of her high chair.

Madison turned in Carly's direction, a soft smile tilting her lips. "She's beautiful," she said. "How old?"

"Two and a half," Dylan answered.

"Will your wife be joining us tonight as well?"

Dylan's back teeth ground together. If she thought he was

hitting on her during the charter trip, being married would make him an even bigger slimebag. "I'm not married."

"Oh, I—I'm sorry." She winced at the gaffe.

"Don't be." He waved a hand dismissively. "I'm not."

"Well, Carly is adorable," Madison added, after an awkward pause.

"And the light of Grandma's life." Ronnie bustled into the room with a basket filled with thick slices of homemade bread. "Glad you could join us, Madison."

Madison rose to take the basket from Ronnie and placed it on the table. "I was surprised to discover Dylan was your son."

Ronnie's eyebrows rose until they almost disappeared beneath her bangs. "Did I forget to tell you that? Heavens, I can't believe it slipped my mind."

Dylan snorted, then covered it up with a mild coughing fit. He didn't believe it, either.

"Now you two sit down and get reacquainted while I get the rest of dinner." She placed a scrap of bread on Carly's tray and disappeared into the kitchen once again.

Reacquainted? They'd barely met twelve hours ago. Madison returned to her seat as Dylan took the chair opposite her.

An awkward silence stretched between them, almost palpable in its discomfort. Madison was doing everything in her power to avoid eye contact. Dylan took the opportunity to look her over more closely.

She'd showered since returning from the charter trip; her shoulder-length blonde hair was sleek and styled once again. Her dress was nice, but far too fancy for Westport. Everything about her screamed, "Big City".

Which was another reason to avoid his mother's matchmaking plans. He and city girls were like oil and water. No, if and when he decided to settle down again, he'd find a small-town sweetheart, one who understood the quirks and foibles of Westport and loved it anyway.

There was no reason to waste his time on an obvious city slicker like Madison.

Unfortunately, his mother didn't share his aversion to the cosmopolitan type.

The matchmaker in question reappeared in the doorway from the kitchen, holding a pot of homemade soup. She set it on a trivet in the center of the table and scooted back into the kitchen. A roast soon joined the soup and bread, followed by a dish of grilled vegetables and a fruit plate.

Good Lord, she was in full tilt Martha Stewart overdrive.

His mother scurried around the table, artfully arranging the food on their plates and fussing over her guest. Madison looked a bit overwhelmed by the attention, but a shy smile played at the corners of her lips.

And even after a morning of extreme seasickness, she managed to eat every bite on her plate, exclaiming over the food as if she'd never had a home-cooked meal.

That was probably the case, he thought. She seemed like the nouvelle cuisine type. Although she didn't turn her nose up at a roast like his ex-wife had been known to do. Instead, she savored the entire meal.

No doubt about it, Madison McIntyre was a study in contrasts. Prim and proper, with a nose so high in the air she'd drown in a strong rainstorm, she came across like a snob of the first order. But she'd managed to survive an Edwards' family meal without a single snippy remark.

A flicker of movement caught his attention and he turned just in time to watch his darling, innocent daughter launch a wad of mashed potatoes at Madison. The white, gooey mess slapped wetly against her neck and slid down the front of her dress.

Dimly, he heard his mother's gasp, but he focused on Madison.

She was looking down, brushing ineffectually at the glob of potato. "I guess now is a good time to ask directions to the bathroom," she said. She looked at Ronnie then, and to Dylan's surprise, she was smiling. A real smile, not one of those "party face" smiles he'd gotten used to when Karen was still around.

No, this was a full-on, eye-crinkling, teeth-gleaming grin that lit her face up like fireworks on the fourth of July. The impact hit him square in the gut, a rush of desire that nearly knocked him out of his chair.

He shook his head, stunned at his own response. Hadn't he learned his lesson? Didn't he know what kind of a woman she was—and what she thought of him? Been there, done that, he reminded his unruly libido.

But a tiny pocket of his brain was sorry that Madison McIntyre would never smile for him in quite the same way.

Madison opened the door to her cabin and slipped inside. It was dark already; she'd spent more time at the Edwards' than she had planned.

But the warmth and welcome at Ronnie's table kept her there even after the last dish had been cleared.

Well, Ronnie was warm and welcoming. And little Carly had charmed her from the moment she laid eyes on her, even with the baptism-by-potato incident. Carly's daddy, however, was a different story.

Madison groaned and dropped down on her bed, scrubbing at her overtired eyes. Horrified didn't come close to describing how she'd felt when she realized that Dylan was Ronnie's son. Even now, a flush of embarrassment washed over her. Here she'd been consoling herself that she wouldn't have to run into him again during her stay, and he was living in the house next door.

Which meant she'd probably see him all the time. Walking on the property. Checking messages at the front desk. He'd probably even be responsible for taking care of handyman chores around the place.

A mental image of Dylan in tight jeans and no shirt, bare chest gleaming with sweat, a leather toolbelt riding low on his hips, flashed through her mind. And then decided to stick around for a while.

Unfortunately, as tantalizing as that image was, Madison couldn't erase the cool disinterest in her fantasy-Dylan's eyes.

After this morning's fiasco, there was no way Dylan would ever warm up to her.

Not that she wanted him to, of course. She was only here for a month, after all, and her time in Westport was reserved for business. As attractive as he was, she just wasn't the type for a holiday fling. And he wasn't her type at all.

She needed someone with ambition, someone stable. Not a live-it-up risk taker. No matter how good-looking he was, she wasn't falling into the same trap as her mother.

She sighed and pushed up from the bed, kicking off her shoes and gathering a nightgown and robe. Time to take off her potato-crusted dress and get comfortable.

In the meantime, she had to remind herself that the things she'd said this morning had only been confirmed by discovering he was Ronnie's son. He was a grown man, and yet he lived with his mother, probably relying on her for free childcare while he goofed off. Not the mature and dependable sort she needed in her life.

No matter how tempted she might be.

Chapter Three

B y eight o'clock the following morning, Madison was ensconced on a sidewalk bench across from the docks, sipping a latte and "researching". An open notebook rested on the bench next to her, but only a few scribbles graced the otherwise-blank page.

The sidewalks were practically empty, although cars lined the main street. Their owners were probably out fishing. Madison suppressed a shudder. She didn't envy them a bit.

Other than the early-morning charter fishing crowds, Westport seemed to get moving later than Seattle. Madison looked around at the empty streets once again, foot tapping impatiently against the leg of the bench.

Picking up the notebook, she jotted down a few more reminders. The harbor was definitely deep enough for cruise liners and ocean-going luxury boats, but the docks would have to be completely reconfigured. And, of course, at least half the fishing boats would have to go.

The street along the docks would need a complete overhaul as well. Madison flipped the page over and sketched a few rough designs for the shops and restaurants that would fill the area, giving the downtown a consistent, upscale appearance.

And the strip of land at the end of the harbor, currently home to an RV park and modest little motel, would be transformed into upper-end condominiums that took advantage of the stellar ocean view.

It was perfect for Donovan Developments—upscale, trendy, catering to the ultra-wealthy. So why did she feel so dissatisfied with the idea?

Sighing again, Madison set the notebook aside. She dug in her bag for a moment or two, finally pulling out her cell phone and hitting speed dial. At the voice mail prompt, she connected to Lily's direct line.

"Maddie! How are you surviving out there in podunk?"

Madison chuckled and shifted the phone to her other ear. "Surviving about covers it."

Lily's sigh could be heard clearly over the line. "I'm so sorry, Maddie. You didn't deserve this treatment."

Madison tapped her pen on the open notebook. "It's a chance to prove myself."

"And that's exactly what you'll do," Lily said, although a note of pity was in her voice.

Great. Now even her best friend was feeling sorry for her. "Look, when I come back to Donovan's with the plans finalized, they won't have any choice but to promote me."

"So tell me," Lily said, not-so-subtly changing the subject, "how is life in a coastal town?"

"Damp," Madison said. "Damp, and salty, and pretty much empty at the moment."

"Feeling lonely, huh? No hunky men to keep you warm at night?"

"You know me better than that," Madison hedged, sure that

Lily would pounce like a kitten on a catnip mouse if she knew about Dylan.

"Unfortunately, yes. You wouldn't notice a gorgeous man if he was dipped in chocolate and left on your pillow. You're too focused on work, work, work. Take my advice, Mad—look around you. There has got to be someone who catches your eye, even in a small town like Westport."

Madison played with the plastic lid on her drink. "I'm here on business, Lily. Besides, I'm not interested in a fling."

"Why on earth not? You're in a new place, nobody knows you, and you probably won't ever go back. It's the perfect opportunity. Go down to the beach and catch yourself a surfer, Maddie. Live a little."

"Don't you have work to do?"

"Don't you?" Lily countered.

"Absolutely. That's why I called. I need some information on the previous Westport attempts. I was sent here so quickly I didn't have time to go through the files. I want to make sure I don't repeat the same mistakes."

Lily sighed again. "So that's it, huh? And I was hoping to live vicariously through you."

"Maybe in another lifetime," Madison said. "Now, how soon can you email me the files?"

Dylan squinted in the dim light of the Westport Public Library. He nodded a greeting to Mrs. Sykes, the librarian, and wound his way to the children's section.

Three train books, one doggie book and a baby music video later, he walked back through the stacks to the checkout counter.

In the far corner, tucked in next to the vertical files, a golden-haired figure bent over a table covered in paperwork.

His pulse kicked up a notch before he could tell his libido to heel. Man, that woman did something to him! Of course, it was purely physical. Just an involuntary reaction left over from caveman days.

Too bad she didn't have the personality to match her looks.

And, yes, he was a big enough man to admit she was good looking. He studied her, taking advantage of her concentration to take a more leisurely look.

Her sun-tinted hair fell in soft waves around her shoulders. Her skin was smooth and delicate-looking, even under the harsh lighting of the ancient library building. And her long lashes fanned out against her cheeks, giving her an oddly delicate air.

But that beautiful exterior held a character that was snobbish, rude, and cold. The original ice princess.

He took a step towards the door. Then another. Then his traitorous feet developed a mind of their own and took a ninety-degree turn and brought him to the edge of her worktable.

It would have been rude to run out without saying hi. She was a guest in his mother's bed and breakfast. He was being polite, that's all. "Working hard, I see."

The effect on Madison was startling, to say the least. Her head shot up, a classic "deer in headlights" look across her porcelain features. With one hand, she slammed the file folder in front of her shut. Then she leaned forward, shielding the rest of her papers from view.

Coincidentally, the protective gesture gave Dylan a clear view of Madison's cleavage. The upper curve of her breasts pushed daringly against the neckline of her scoop neck t-shirt. He blinked, startled by her odd behavior as well as her unknowingly seductive pose.

"Harboring state secrets?" He lifted one eyebrow at the flustered Ms. McIntyre. An attractive blush tinted her face and neck, even adding a pink glow to the pale skin of her chest.

"You startled me," she muttered, pulling herself upright and closing folders with alarming speed. "I'm just catching up on some work."

"Mom said you were on sabbatical," he replied, casting his glance over the upside-down papers before she hid them from view. "You're working pretty hard for someone on vacation."

"Some of us are dedicated to our work." She began stacking the closed folders in tidy piles.

"Some of us know how to balance our work and our personal lives," Dylan retorted. Of course, his mother would argue he wasn't one of them, but at least he didn't put in a full day's work on vacation, for heaven's sake.

Madison glared at him. "Aren't you supposed to be driving the boat or something right now?"

"Captaining the ship, and no, we caught our quota early today. I'm just picking up some reading material for Carly before I head home."

She stood and leaned over, peering at his selections with interest. "Isn't she too young to read?"

"Yes, but not too young to be read to. I figure by the time she hits kindergarten we'll have plowed through the entire picture book section of the library."

"Good for you."

Dylan looked at her sharply, but found only respect and approval in her gaze.

She smiled at him, then glanced back down at the files on the desk in front of her. "Well, I should get back to—my project."

"Okay," Dylan said, shifting the books under his arm. "I guess I'll see you back at The Inn."

The corners of her mouth turned up briefly. Then she pulled another folder out of her briefcase and began flipping through the pages enclosed.

He could take a hint. Dylan turned and walked out the door into the sunshine.

Fool.

Idiot, cretin, numskull.

She could think of another dozen choice words, but Madison was too much of a lady to use them. Even when the subject was herself.

It was possible that she could have acted more idiotically in Dylan's presence, but at the moment she couldn't think of a single way that could have occurred. Flinging herself across the papers as if they were ablaze—oh, yeah, really smooth move. Way to be discreet.

A quick glance at the clock above the checkout counter revealed that time had passed more swiftly than she'd expected. It was well past lunchtime, and now that her stomach had been reminded of that fact it began protesting. Loudly.

Madison stacked the rest of her paperwork in her briefcase and walked out of the library. She squinted in the bright sunlight, shading her eyes with her free hand. Dropping the briefcase on the passenger seat, she rounded the car and got in.

One of the nice things about a small town, she mused, was the short distance between points of interest. Less than a minute on the road and she was pulling into a parking spot in front of the Seafood Shack Café.

The scent of fried fish drifted out the open door, and Madison inhaled deeply. Now this was how fish was meant to be experienced—already caught, cleaned, cooked, and ready to eat. Her stomach grumbled again, so she hitched her purse over her shoulder and stepped inside.

A lunch counter took up the right-hand side of the tiny café, with the kitchen directly behind and a handful of tables hugging the opposite wall. Even a couple of hours past lunchtime, the place was full, and the noise level momentarily stopped Madison in her tracks.

She hung back, uncertain, as a wave of sensory overload washed over her. Slowly, she realized that the noise level had drastically reduced as the patrons of the café turned to check out the new arrival.

Madison could feel the flush of embarrassment climbing her neck, and she took an involuntary step backward. Suddenly, she felt a hand on her elbow.

"Come on, I've got a table in the back." Dylan patiently steered her forward and seated her in the high-back booth near the back exit.

The lull in conversation around him had alerted Dylan to Madison's arrival. Her fresh-from-the-city outfit drew the attention of the regulars at the Seafood Shack, and her shining good looks kept that attention past the point of her own comfort. She had looked about ready to bolt and, impulsively, he stepped in to help out.

Dylan wasn't sure why he kept finding excuses to interact with Madison. She was everything he had made it a point to avoid. But something drew him to her anyway.

"You didn't have to do that," she said, her chin tilted defiantly.

"Do what?" Dylan crossed his arms and leaned back in the booth.

"Rescue me." She waved a hand dismissively at the front of the café. "I'm not a damsel in distress. I am perfectly capable of eating lunch by myself."

Dylan leaned forward, planting his hands on the table in front of him. "And I'm not a knight in shining armor. I'm just a guy who saw one of his mother's clients and offered to share his table in a full restaurant. Excuse me for being thoughtful."

Madison shrank back a little, her gaze dropping. "I'm sorry. I didn't mean to be so…"

"Touchy?" Dylan shrugged, not quite willing to let go of his annoyance just yet. "I'm used to it."

"What's that supposed to mean?" She straightened again.

Case in point. "Nothing. You just seem a little high strung today."

If the heat behind her glare could have been measured, it would have broken the thermometer. "Thanks for your insight. Now, if you'll excuse me…"

Dylan reached out and covered her hand with his, stopping her move to leave. "Look, let's start over. The café is busy today. Would you like to join me for lunch?"

Madison glared at him for a few moments longer, then smiled sheepishly. "Thank you very much. I'd be happy to join you. And I promise not to bite your head off again." Then she gently tugged her hand out from under his and sat back down.

Dylan was oddly disconcerted at the loss of her touch. His hand felt empty somehow, as if an important connection was missing. He shook off the sensation and handed her a menu.

She studied it intently, a small furrow between her eyes. "Everything is so…"

"Greasy?"

"I was going to say fattening," she chided.

"Same difference," he said with a grin.

They both jumped as an order pad slapped down on the table between them. "Dylan Edwards, you are officially on my bad side now," growled the woman standing at the side of the table. "Calling my food greasy, and in front of a visitor to boot!"

Dylan rose and planted a kiss on the buxom woman's cheek. "No offense intended, Sal. You know I prefer your grease over pretty much everything."

"Better not let your mother hear you say that," she teased. "So, are you going to introduce me to your date?"

Dylan opened his mouth to protest, but Madison beat him to the punch. "Oh, no. I'm not his date. I'm just staying at his mother's bed and breakfast." She held out her hand. "Madison McIntyre."

"Nice to meet you, Madison," replied the woman, casting a disbelieving look at Dylan. "I'm Sallie. Owner, cook and head waitress of the Seafood Shack. And Dylan has never eaten lunch here with anyone from his mom's B and B."

"I brought someone in just last week, Sallie," Dylan protested, which earned him a whack upside the head with her order pad.

"Your daughter doesn't count," Sallie said. "She's adorable, but she's still family."

A quick glance at Madison informed him that she was as uncomfortable with the direction of the conversation as he was. A pink tint colored her cheeks. He cleared his throat and handed his menu to Sallie with a pointed glare.

She took the hint. "So what'll you two have?" Her pencil hovered over the green and white order pad.

"The usual," Dylan said. To Madison, he clarified, "Fish and chips with a side of prawns."

Madison pressed her lips together, studying the menu as if it were written in Sanskrit. "I'll have the house salad."

"No, you won't." Dylan met Madison's startled look with a quick shake of the head. "Skip the salad. Have the fish and chips, at least a small basket. It's the house specialty."

Madison narrowed her eyes at him, but finally handed her menu to Sallie. "I'll defer to the regular customer."

Dylan waited for Sallie to leave their table before leaning over and whispering, "She's had the same bag of salad in the fridge since the Nixon Administration. At this restaurant, stick with the fried foods."

"That's the second rescue in one day," Madison noted. A glimmer of amusement sparkled in her eyes. "You may have to rethink that whole knight in shining armor thing."

"I don't think so," Dylan said, stretching his arm across the back of the booth. "Metal isn't really a good fashion choice on the coast."

"Too uncomfortable?"

He shook his head. "Rusts too easily."

She tossed her head back and laughed. "I can just see it. You head outside one night to rescue a damsel in distress, and end up frozen on the front lawn like the Tin Man."

He rolled his eyes. "Just don't expect me to break into song anytime soon."

"Not a singer?"

"The only way you'd ever hear me sing is if you were in the shower with me."

Surprisingly, her face pinkened a little at that comment. Was the city girl actually blushing?

Any why in the world was he bringing showers into the conversation, for heaven's sake?

Now he'd managed to plant the image in his head, and with his luck it would decide to stick around for a while. Madison naked, standing under the shower spray, suds trailing down her body in rivulets of bubbles. Reaching out to touch her soap-slick skin, pulling her closer...

Oh, God. He was in trouble.

At least he had a good excuse not to leave just yet. Standing up at this point would be pretty damn embarrassing.

Now, if only they had something to interrupt the awkward

silence that had descended on their table. He glanced over at Madison. Was she struggling with the same erotic thoughts that were currently plaguing him?

He wasn't sure if he wanted the answer to be yes, or no. He'd sworn off women—especially women like Madison—when his marriage had imploded.

But there was something about Madison that was—tempting.

Before he could explore that particular train of thought any further, Sallie appeared at his elbow and slid baskets of fish and chips across the table. "Here you go," she said, pulling a bottle of ketchup out of the pocket of her voluminous apron.

"It looks amazing," Madison said, shaking out her napkin.

Sallie beamed. "If you don't think it's the best fish and chips you've ever had, I'll eat my apron."

Madison broke off a piece of fish and popped it in her mouth. "Your apron is safe," she said, turning to Sallie with a smile. "It's fantastic."

"Told ya." Sal winked at her and turned to go. "Enjoy your meal, kids," she tossed over her shoulder on her way to the kitchen.

"Wow." Madison took another bite. "This gives my favorite fish and chips a run for its money."

"I thought you didn't eat fish and chips."

She wrinkled her nose. "I shouldn't. My hips are not happy when I eat fried foods. But fish and chips have always been one of my favorites."

Huh. And he'd pegged her as a sushi type.

Dylan swallowed and looked away. If he wasn't careful, he might actually start to like Madison McIntyre. And for his own well-being, that's the last thing he wanted to do.

Dusk had crept into the cabin when Madison wasn't looking. She glanced up from the papers spread out on her bed and reached over to switch on the gooseneck lamp on the night-stand. A soft glow chased away the shadows and gave the cozy room a cheerful cast.

She sighed, rubbing the back of her neck and stretching out the kinks in her back. Any more time reviewing these files and she'd start seeing double.

Madison closed the folder in her lap and pushed it onto the comforter. She now had a better idea what *not* to do when approaching Westport about the resort—but absolutely no idea what to do instead.

Simply put, nothing had worked. Financial incentives, flashy presentations, chatting up the locals—all the traditional avenues had been dead ends.

The worst part was, Madison needed the cooperation of the town if this resort was ever going to get off the ground. The main piece of land coveted by Donovan Development Company was owned by the town itself, in a public trust that required the approval of the city council. So far, it had been emphatically not for sale. Rumor had it that certain city council members were adamant about saving the property from development. Unless she could convince the town that selling the property was in the best interests of Westport, this project was dead in the water.

Much like her personal life.

Madison frowned at the turn of her thoughts. It wasn't like she'd given up a thriving social life when she'd decided to focus her energy completely on her job. Hired straight out of college, she'd attacked work with the same single-mindedness that got her a stellar GPA in school.

Unfortunately, the business world hadn't been as kind as the world of academia. Used to working hard and keeping her head down, Madison had found herself ostracized by the tight-knit group of employees.

Particularly Bob, the rising star of Donovan Development, who had taken every opportunity to point out what a poor "team player" she was. Especially after she'd refused to "play" with him after hours.

Lily, her one ally in the entire company, had warned her that when Bob was promoted to management he'd find a way to make life difficult for her.

She'd just never imagined he'd send her to Westport to do it.

Oh, he could couch it as a "wonderful challenge," a "great opportunity." But she knew that he was rubbing his hands with glee at the prospect of her failure.

So she couldn't fail. It wasn't an option. Just because no one else had been able to find a way to push this resort through didn't mean it was impossible. All she had to do was work a little harder, that's all.

And if thoughts of Dylan—naked, in the shower—kept intruding, she'd just have to banish them. Somehow.

Madison tapped the edges of the stack of papers in front of her, trying to line them up more precisely. Lily teased her about being a neat freak, but there was something comforting about everything being just right.

Order. Discipline. Focus. They had been a source of comfort and structure in her life for as long as she could remember. But she was starting to get the sinking feeling that even they couldn't rescue her from this mess.

What she really wanted right now was a chance to relax, even if only for a short time. The prospect of a true sabbatical filled her with a wistfulness she didn't even realize she possessed.

Explore the town for fun, not "research". Spend time on the beach.

Get to know a certain fishing boat captain who floated her boat.

But even as she considered it, Madison rejected the idea out of hand. She had to stay focused on her responsibilities, not fun and games. Her job had to remain first, last, and in between. Like it had ever since she'd joined Donovan Development.

In fact, with the daunting prospect of the development deal from H-E-double chopsticks, combined with the temptation inherent in any dealings with Dylan Edwards, Madison was tempted to shut herself in her room indefinitely.

At least here she'd be safe from failure—and from the emotions Dylan churned up in her.

Chapter Four

Dylan sat back in the porch swing, Carly tucked against him as they swayed. She rubbed a bit of fuzz under her nose while she sucked her thumb—a charming, if slightly odd, habit that popped up when she was tired.

The sun was starting to set; although he couldn't see the horizon from the front porch, a pink tinge colored the sky. And the muted roar of the ocean wrapped around him like a comfortable quilt.

Carly snuggled closer and sighed heavily, her eyes sinking shut. It was past her bedtime, but Dylan had wanted just a little more Daddy Time tonight.

The fish hadn't been biting today; he'd had to stay out the maximum time on *The Lucky Strike* just to ensure his customers a reasonable catch. Then a malfunction in the fish finder kept him on the docks well past his usual return.

The fishing season was a difficult time for him now that Carly was in his life. During the off-season, he was a hands-on parent, taking on the daily rituals of raising a child with enthusiasm. But when the fish were running, he was limited to afternoons and early evenings.

He had it better than a lot of his charter-fishing compatriots, he knew. Many of them had to fish in Alaska during the fall and winter just to keep the creditors at bay. He winced at the thought of leaving Carly behind for months at a time. Luckily, he'd never had to make that choice.

Dylan kissed the top of Carly's head, grateful once again that Karen hadn't bothered to fight him for custody. She'd never been particularly interested in being a parent, and when the opportunity to leave Westport arose, she grabbed it without a backward glance. He didn't see how anyone could abandon their child, but that was only one of the things about his ex-wife he didn't understand.

A crunching noise alerted him to the presence of another person. With the crushed-rock pathway, no one could walk past without being noticed.

He looked up and swallowed a sigh. Of course it was Madison.

He'd managed to avoid her for two days now, ever since their impromptu lunch at the Seafood Shack. His unwanted attraction for her was growing stronger, and he hoped that out-of-sight, out-of-mind would nip it in the bud.

Unfortunately, his mind hadn't cooperated, replaying images of Madison throughout his waking hours. Her startled look as he approached her in the library. The grin on her face when Carly tagged her with mashed potatoes. The way her khakis clung to every curve after a dousing on *The Lucky Strike*.

Even their innocent lunch together had provided ammunition for his libido. She'd spilled cocktail sauce down the side of her hand and lapped it up with a perfect pink tongue. Only in his fantasy his tongue had been doing the lapping.

Dylan shifted in his seat, wishing he was anywhere but out here, in the gathering darkness, Madison walking slowly down the path in front of him.

Carly whimpered and sucked her thumb more vigorously. Startled, Dylan realized that she had fallen asleep, rocked gently by the motion of the porch swing. Quietly, he gathered her in his arms and stood.

The movement must have caught Madison's eye, because she stopped walking and turned in his direction. He motioned her quiet with a finger to his lips, and she nodded. Then Dylan turned and carried Carly into the house.

It was several minutes before he returned to the porch, expecting it to be empty. But a slim figure had taken his spot in the porch swing and was rocking it back and forth with a tennis-shoe-clad foot.

She looked up as he stepped onto the porch. "I hope you don't mind," she said softly, indicating the swing with a tilt of her head.

"No, no," he replied, although a part of him did. So much for peace of mind tonight.

He leaned against the porch rail opposite Madison, watching her swing. She sat with her head tilted back, squinting through the twilight at the first stars peeking through.

"I was hoping I might see you tonight."

"You were?" Dylan tamped down the little hitch of desire. Had he learned nothing from his disaster of a marriage? Besides, she thought he was a resort-town playboy. She had probably decided she wanted a vacation fling, after all.

That burst of excitement turned sour in his stomach.

"Yes," she continued, obviously unaware of the turn of his thoughts. "I was hoping to get your input."

"My...input?" Dylan turned a quizzical look towards her. "Input about what?"

"Real estate." The comment hung in the air between them, almost as palpable as a cartoon speech bubble. Dylan fought the urge to check his ears for water.

"Real estate?" he repeated, annoyed at how he was starting to sound like a parrot.

"I'm looking for some information on property in Westport. I was hoping you could recommend a realtor in the area."

"If you don't mind my asking, why are you interested in real estate in Westport?"

Madison looked down at her linked hands. "Just curious."

On impulse, Dylan reached out and snagged her chin, lifting her head until her eyes met his.

Big mistake. Huge. Now he was in actual physical contact with the woman he'd been avoiding for days. His pulse rate tripled and his breathing grew shallow. He was rocked by the desire to lean forward and cover her mouth with his.

She felt it, too, if the racing pulse beneath his fingertips was any indication. She swayed toward him, lips slightly parted, her eyes wide and unmoving.

He dropped his hand, fingertips tingling from the brief contact with her smooth skin. He shrugged, faking a nonchalance he didn't actually feel. "No offense, but I don't believe you."

Fire flashed in her blue eyes, followed by something less identifiable. Was it—fear? Then both emotions were gone, replaced by that cool, superior gaze he'd first seen on the charter trip. "Excuse me?"

"Nobody is 'just curious' about real estate in Westport, least of all you."

"Why not?" Her chin tilted up defiantly.

Dylan held up his hand, ticking off the reasons on his fingers. "It's a small town miles from anywhere. There's little in the way of job prospects other than fishing and logging, and both are tricky professions at best. There are no department stores, no fancy coffee houses, no upscale restaurants. There is nothing in this town to interest a person like you."

Madison reached out and placed a hand on his forearm, cutting off any other reasons. Of course, with her delicate hand burning a brand into his arm, the rest of his arguments vanished from thought.

"A person like me?" Her eyes were darker, more serious, if that was even possible.

"A city girl," he answered honestly. "Someone used to city life wouldn't fit in out here in the boondocks. You'd get bored after a while and run back home."

She nodded slowly, her eyes never leaving his face. An odd look of disappointment flitted across her features before she schooled them again. "I see," she murmured.

Dylan fought the urge to apologize. All he'd done was tell her the truth.

"Well, if you must know, I'm not asking for myself. I'm doing some research for my—my mother."

Odd, how she stumbled over that phrase. Dylan wondered if there was more to her 'research' than she was willing to share. Something just didn't sit right with this conversation.

"Your mother is interested in Westport?" He played along, hoping she'd trip over some detail and reveal more than she intended.

"Actually, any small town to retire in," she said. "I'm just starting here because this is where I'm—on sabbatical."

That pause again. Dylan crossed his arms and waited.

He didn't have to wait long.

"I have the time, and she doesn't, so I'm doing a little preliminary research for her. You know, the good daughter and all." She twisted a corner of her light yellow cardigan between her fingers.

More silence.

"That's what I was working on. You know, in the library. When we ran into each other the other day." She twisted the cardigan more tightly.

Dylan lifted an eyebrow.

"So, anyway, do you have any? Suggestions, I mean?" *Twist, twist.* Nervous tension was rolling off her in waves.

"Yeah, I have a suggestion." He crossed his arms. "Try Surfside instead."

"Surfside?"

Dylan nodded. "About forty-five miles up the coast. It's a perfect retirement location. Developers got hold of it a decade or so ago, and it's definitely more upscale." He spit the word out as if it left a bad taste in his mouth.

"I take it you don't approve?"

"Surfside used to be a nice, quiet town. Now it's overrun with condos, fancy shops, and overpriced restaurants."

"Some people like that," she argued.

"Sure, but the effects on the town have been devastating. Property taxes have skyrocketed. Long-time residents have lost their homes. And the environment has been destroyed by over-building. I don't ever want that to happen to Westport."

Madison was quiet. Eyes averted, she bit her lip.

Dylan took pity on her. "Sorry. I get a little wound up on the subject."

"I noticed." She flashed a weak smile.

"Hey, if you're still interested, one of Mom's friends is a realtor. She's got an office down on the docks. I can get one of her cards from the front desk."

Relief washed across her face. "Thank you. I'd really appreciate it."

He excused himself and walked into the house, grateful for the opportunity to compose himself before continuing his conversation with Madison. He rummaged through the drawers in his mother's desk, finally locating the business cards under a stack of "to-be-filed" paperwork.

He took one and walked slowly to the door. Madison was on the other side, waiting for him.

Or more precisely, waiting for what she could get from him. And experience had taught Dylan to be wary of women like that.

No matter how tempting the exterior packaging might be.

Madison wandered down the pathway, the white rocks visible in the filtered moonlight. The fog had rolled out tonight almost as quickly as it had rolled in, leaving a clear night sky laced with the sharp scent of seawater.

She gripped her cardigan, suppressing a shiver. Although there was a bite to the air, it wasn't the cool temperature making her tremble.

Her hand slipped into her pocket, running a finger over the slightly raised type on the realtor's card. She fought the urge to check if it still carried Dylan's scent.

Once Dylan had returned with the card she had ended their conversation, murmuring a polite thank you before high-tailing it off the porch as quickly as good manners would allow.

Even now, a good fifteen minutes after leaving, her nerves were still jangling. Her cozy little cabin suddenly seemed much too confining, so she decided to keep walking the property until her head was clear.

Lily was right. She'd been out of circulation for far too long—if she'd ever *been* in circulation, that is. Shy and awkward around the opposite sex, she'd never been one for the dating scene. Her only serious relationship, in college, had ended badly when he decided her roommate was more fun than she was. And Madison, buried under a double classload and family obligations, had been chagrined to realize he was right. That had ended her dating career, in college and beyond.

It was easier to throw herself into work and avoid the whole male/female issue altogether.

But when she was around Dylan, Madison couldn't avoid it. The attraction she felt for him traveled through her veins like electricity singing in high-voltage wires. It was a feeling unlike any she had experienced before.

Of course, she had precious little experience in that arena. But still, the temptation was there.

And she had no idea what to do about it.

Madison wandered down the path, barely noting the direction her feet were taking. There was a point tonight, when she and Dylan were talking, that she was sure he was going to kiss her. He'd taken her chin in his hand, and only a slight movement forward would have caused their lips to connect.

She'd sat there, heart pounding, willing him to kiss her. Madison didn't think she'd ever wanted anything so much in her entire life.

And then he had moved away.

Her face still burned with mortification. She must have read the signals wrong. Heaven knows she'd been doing that since they met.

And he'd been totally upfront about his opinion of her. It was just painful to hear it spelled out so coldly. She sighed, fingering the business card again. Once again, her innate shyness and fear of the unknown had translated itself into being a snob.

Usually, she just buried herself in work and convinced herself that she didn't care what anyone thought of her. But

Dylan's opinion seemed to be carrying more weight than she would have imagined.

Which was going to make it even more difficult when the truth came out about her purpose for being in Westport. She'd sat there in the porch swing tonight, cringing at his disgust over the development in Surfside. The fact that Donovan's chief rival had been responsible for that project–and that Donovan planned to out-glitz Surfside with their Westport resort–made it even worse.

Well, she'd cross that bridge when she came to it.

She looked around, suddenly realizing that in her introspective state she'd completely lost track of her location. The evergreens towered over her, blocking all but the slimmest bit of moonlight. The ankle-high path lights illuminated her feet and little else. Although the crushed white rock reassured her she hadn't left the property, she still felt anxiety building in the darkness.

A heavy footstep behind her sent her heart leaping into her throat. She whirled, instinctively crouching in the "position of strength" drilled into her by the self-defense coach she'd taken lessons from a few years back.

"Hey, take it easy. It's only me."

But 'only' wasn't a word Madison would use to describe Dylan. Especially the way he looked right now.

Clad in a pair of swim trunks and little else, he stood right in the middle of the walkway, gripping the ends of the towel that was looped around his neck. His bare chest, dappled by moonlight, was an appealing combination of planes and shadows. The taut muscles of his abdomen were obviously the result of a life of physical activity. His legs were lean and toned, lightly furred with the same dark hair curling on his chest.

Madison realized that she was staring and ripped her gaze away. "Sorry. I guess I overreacted." She slowly came out of her self-defense pose, grateful that the darkness of night hid her flaming blush.

"Hey, better safe than sorry. I was just going to the hot tub for a soak." He indicated the swim trunks.

"There's a hot tub?"

He grinned, his even white teeth gleaming in the darkness. "So much for that full-color brochure Mom insisted on. Didn't you even read the promotional materials?"

Madison shook her head. "Sorry."

"Hey, don't apologize to me. Just don't mention it to Mom. She thinks her new PR campaign is the reason you picked The Inn for your sabbatical."

Madison winced as her lie rolled off his tongue. The harder she worked to convince the people around her that she was on vacation, the worse it was going to be when the truth came out. Well, there was nothing she could do about it now.

"Actually, the website did the trick."

"You liked it?" He was standing even with her now, a subtle tension in the air between them that she couldn't begin to explain.

"No, my friend Lily did." At his puzzled look, she hastened to explain. "The–sabbatical was a last-minute decision. I had barely any time to prepare. She researched the area and made the reservations for me. I do remember her saying that The Inn looked like the nicest place in Westport, though."

"Well, tell your friend Lily thanks for the vote of confidence."

"So, did your Mom hire a hotshot designer to create this website?"

He shrugged, glancing away. "A local."

"Well, he or she must have done a fabulous job. Lily was very impressed." She stopped, tipping her head back and looking up at the deep-velvet-blue night sky. "I can't believe how dark it gets here."

"No city lights to get in the way," Dylan said. He walked back to where she stood, lacing his fingers through hers and tugging her forward. "Come on. But be careful. The path can be tricky at night. You don't want to trip."

"Trip on what?" she asked, but he just gripped her hand more tightly. And then she was so wrapped up in the delicious sensation of holding hands with a half-naked, gorgeous man than she forgot to question anything at all.

"Here we are." Dylan swept his free hand in front of him. The crushed rock path ended a few steps ahead of them, giving way to a meadow circled by evergreens. At the far corner, a hill-side sloped gently. Steam rose invitingly from the rocks.

Madison sighed, entranced by the view.

"The hot tub is built into the hillside, using all natural materials. It's made to look as organic as possible."

"Then it's definitely a success." She cast a sideways glance at him. "So how far are we from the cabins?"

His thumb was stroking lazy circles on the back of her hand. "Not as far as you'd think. You took the roundabout path on your walk."

"I needed to clear my head a bit."

Dylan nodded. "How's your head now?"

She thought for a moment before answering. "Better, I think."

"Good." He squeezed her hand and let go, leaving her to mourn the loss of contact. "Well, I have to be up early tomorrow, so I'm going to take a dip."

"Then I guess I'll see you later." She took a halting step backwards.

He nodded and started walking across the meadow. He stopped a few paces in. "You're welcome to join me, you know.

Just go get your suit on and take the main path back through the cabins."

For a moment she was tempted. The thought of sinking into steaming water with this attractive, unpredictable man was enough to make her stomach clench and goosebumps appear on every exposed inch of flesh.

Then good sense intruded. "Sorry," she murmured, shaking her head. "I don't have a swimsuit with me."

His eyes met hers, full of heat and challenge. "No suit?" The simple phrase held a wealth of innuendo that caused Madison's blush to rage even hotter. "Hmm. Too bad. Maybe next time, then."

And with a noncommittal mumble, Madison turned away and fled to the safety of her room.

Chapter Five

"Good morning!" Ronnie's voice warbled across the dining room. "Come on in and have a seat."

A basket of freshly baked scones took up the center of the table, the aroma tantalizing her. Madison took one, wondering what else Ronnie had in store for breakfast this morning.

She didn't have a scale in her cabin, but she would be amazed if she hadn't put on at least a few pounds after a week of Ronnie's breakfasts. Elegant, rich, and luscious, they were masterpieces of culinary art. Madison couldn't resist them.

Much like she couldn't resist Ronnie's son. No, that wasn't quite right, considering she had resisted him last night. But after a sleepless night tossing and turning, Madison was mortified to admit that she didn't want to resist him any longer.

The trouble was, she knew what he thought of her—he'd been very clear in his dislike of "girls like her." And her behavior on the charter trip had given him a strong impression of her opinion of him.

Too bad she had no idea how to let him know her opinion was changing.

Sighing, she popped a bite of scone into her mouth, savoring the flaky layers. Ronnie was the undisputed master when it came to pastry.

"Good morning!" Dylan strode into the dining room, a cheery grin on his handsome features. He turned the chair at the head of the table around and straddled it, leaning his muscled forearms on the back.

Madison inhaled sharply, remembering too late the bite of scone still in her mouth. Bits of pastry stuck in her throat, causing her to cough uncontrollably. Dylan moved as if to help her, but she waved him back. A few sips of ice water tamed her coughing fit. She could tell that her face was red, courtesy of her near-choking as well as her embarrassment.

Not once in the week she'd been at The Inn had Dylan joined the guests for breakfast. By this hour, he should have been out on *The Lucky Strike*.

Ronnie bustled back into the room, a dish of scrambled eggs and ham in her hands. By the look on her face, she was just as startled to see her son as Madison was.

"Is everything all right? I heard someone coughing."

As if on cue, everyone at the table turned and looked at Madison. She raised her hand half-heartedly, face flaming even brighter. "Sorry. A bit of scone went down the wrong pipe."

"Oh, you poor dear. Here, drink a little water." Although the situation was no longer dire, Madison followed Ronnie's directions. The innkeeper hovered over her until she was satisfied with Madison's recovery. Then her attention shifted to her son.

"Dylan, sit properly in that chair. We have guests."

Madison stifled a grin as Dylan slowly swung the chair

around and sat down again. It was obvious that Ronnie delighted in being the mother hen.

"And why aren't you on the water?"

He reached over and grabbed the coffeepot, pouring himself a mugful before answering. "Weather. I got down to the docks and found out there was a small craft warning for today. I cancelled the trip."

"Wonderful!" Ronnie clapped her hands together. "You have a whole day off!"

Madison caught the suspicious look Dylan shot his mother. Did he think Ronnie was up to something?

Come to think of it, she did look like a kitty with a mouthful of canary feathers. But before Ronnie could speak, Dylan cut her off.

"Yes, I'm really looking forward to a whole day with Carly. Is she awake yet?"

At the mention of the personable toddler the other women at the table cooed, smiling at Dylan as if he'd just announced that he was planning to build an orphanage on the property. Madison fought a smile as Dylan's cheeks reddened under the glare of public attention.

Ronnie shook her head. "Not yet. The poor dear must need her sleep. Someone kept her up late last night," she said, trying to inject a note of censure into her voice and failing miserably.

Dylan shrugged. "Daddy's privilege." He dug into the dish of eggs in front of him and started filling his plate.

The rest of the diners followed his lead, and the attention of the room swiftly focused on the outstanding breakfast. The room was quiet except for the clink of fork on plate and the occasional murmured request for someone to pass a dish.

"Daddy!" Carly burst into the room, a mini-whirlwind in pink footed pajamas. "Daddy home!"

Dylan scooped her into his arms, settling her into his lap with a grin. "Daddy gets to spend the whole day with you, punkin. What do you want to do?"

"Color!" She gripped his cheeks between her chubby palms, staring him in the eye with a serious expression. "Dolls! Beach!"

He kissed her on the forehead and gently pried her fingers away from his face. Turning, he placed her in the high chair at the corner of the table. "Then color, dolls, and beach it is. But first, breakfast." He broke a section of scone into bite-sized pieces and scattered them on Carly's tray.

"Madison?" An elbow tapped her side, startling her out of her reverie. The woman next to her smiled knowingly. "I'm sorry, dear. Mrs. Edwards just asked you a question."

Mortified at being caught daydreaming over Dylan, Madison focused her complete attention on his mother.

"I was just wondering what your plans were for the day," she said, placing a fruit tray on the table.

"Work," she replied automatically, remembering too late that she wasn't supposed to be working at all. Dylan glanced at her, a speculative look in his eye. Stammering, she continued, "I mean working on a project. For my mother. Some research."

"Her mom is thinking of buying some retirement property here in Westport," Dylan added, with a slight quirk to his eyebrow.

"Really!" Ronnie picked up the now-empty scone basket, her face beaming. "I knew you had an ulterior motive for coming to Westport."

Madison smiled weakly and toyed with her food. When they discovered her real motive for being in Westport, their attitude would go south in a hurry.

She was definitely not looking forward to that day.

. . .

Carly was finally down for her nap. Dylan was tempted to follow her lead; their busy morning had pretty much worn him out.

And his day had started at the usual crack of dawn, following a night of unusually poor sleep. He'd thrashed around in his bed, sheets tangling around his legs, unable to shake the dreams that filled his head. No matter how much his logical side insisted Madison was completely wrong for him, his libido begged to differ.

He went in search of his mother, hoping to slip away for a bit while Carly slept. She was more than willing to keep an ear out for her grandbaby while he took a walk. Maybe the brisk wind that had beached the fleet this morning would clear his mind.

Moments later, he was outside on the porch, drinking in the damp, salt-scented wind. The waves would be spectacular down at Washaway Beach.

On impulse, he bounded down the steps and started to walk. He wasn't particularly surprised when he found himself outside Madison's cheery yellow cabin. Of course, he hadn't mentioned that possibility to his mother when he asked for babysitting help. He wasn't a masochist.

If Ronnie Edwards knew where he was right now, she'd be busy picking out china patterns for the two of them before he got back to the main house.

Madison didn't answer his knock right away. The light was on, however, even though it was mid-afternoon, so he figured she was home. He rapped again, a bit louder, on the doorframe.

The door swung open and there she was, framed in the glow of the bedside lamp. Her hair was piled haphazardly on top of her head, secured with a ruffled fabric-covered elastic band. Strands curled around her face, giving it a touchingly fragile look. Tortoiseshell glasses perched on the end of her nose.

With a gasp, she wrenched the glasses off and hid them behind her back, one hand unconsciously patting her disheveled hair. "What are you doing here?"

He grinned despite the less-than-enthusiastic welcome. "Just dropping by to make sure you aren't working too hard."

"There's no such thing," she countered, sidestepping to the table near the door and surreptitiously dropping her glasses on a stack of papers.

"Oh, I don't know about that," he said, taking advantage of her move to enter the tiny cabin. His gaze traveled over the room, taking in the stacks of paperwork and color-coordinated file folders.

Madison noticed his appraisal and hurried over to the bed, picking up stacks of paper and placing them neatly in the cardboard box labeled "Westport". It was quickly filled to overflowing.

"Lots of information for a potential retirement purchase," Dylan observed, leaning one hip against the two-person table in the center of the kitchenette. "Interesting."

Madison's head shot up, her eyes wide. "Why do you say that?"

He shrugged. "Most people would pick up a brochure or two and call it a day."

She bent over her papers again, tucking the last of them into her briefcase. Her face was shadowed in the soft light. "Nobody ever accused me of being an underachiever."

Dylan laughed. "I can believe that." At her narrow-eyed look, he held up a hand. "No offense."

Now it was her turn to shrug. "None taken." But there was a pensive cast to her face.

He waited while she finished cleaning up. The interior of

her cabin was spotless–and not just because his mom took great pride in keeping a tidy establishment. Most other guests who stayed long-term tended to move in after a few days–jacket on the back of a chair, slippers by the bed, a mug drying in the rack by the sink. But other than the tidy stacks of paperwork, nothing in this cabin indicated anyone was staying here at all.

No, that wasn't quite right. The air in the cabin was lightly scented with her perfume. Not quite floral, not quite spicy, it wrapped around his senses like a perfect spring day. He drew in a breath, feeling tension flow out – and a new tension taking its place.

She closed her briefcase with a snap and stood for a moment. Then she sat down at the table, gesturing for Dylan to join her.

"So, the question still stands."

Dylan stared at her, not quite sure what she was talking about.

Madison waved a hand at him. "Why are you here?"

He leaned back in his chair. "I thought you might need a break about now."

"Oh. Well, thank you. This is a nice change of pace."

Dylan snorted. "It figures that you'd consider five minutes of tidying up a break. No, Maddie, you need to get out of this cabin for a while."

She was shaking her head before he even finished the last sentence. "No, thank you. I have too much to do. Besides, isn't this your Carly and Daddy day?"

"She's napping. And what more do you have to work on? You just put everything away."

Madison opened her mouth—to argue, Dylan assumed—and then closed it with a snap.

"Besides, you can consider this research," he cajoled, trying to coax a smile out of her. "You can't give your mother an objective report by studying paperwork. You need to get out and experience Westport for yourself."

"I already tried that," she grumbled. "It was a disaster."

Dylan bit back a smile. "I promise, nothing we do for the next hour will make you want to hurl."

Her lips twitched as she tried to hold on to her scowl, but it was a losing battle. "Well, with a promise like that, how can I say no?"

Madison could hear the roar of the surf even over the car engine. She huddled deeper into her all-weather parka, tugging the collar closer to her ears.

Everywhere else in Western Washington, it was practically summer. In Westport, she was caught in a midwinter storm. But the wind blowing outside the car was nothing compared to the tempest raging inside her.

She glanced sideways, still befuddled by the turn of events. One minute she was hunkered down over paperwork, and the next she was buckled into Dylan's surprisingly practical four-door sedan, headed for who-knew-where.

This wasn't like her.

Secretly, though, she very much wished it was.

She'd barely had time to change clothes, all the while hyper-aware that Dylan was sitting on her bed, on the other side of the bathroom door. Then he'd picked out a coat for her, rolled his eyes at her footwear selection, and escorted her out of the cabin.

"Here we are." Dylan pulled into a tiny parking lot surrounded by scrub pine. He switched off the car and reached over the back of the seat to grab a backpack from the floor of the car. "Ready for an adventure?"

Madison nodded, her mouth suddenly dry. His face was mere inches from hers, the fresh clean masculine scent of his skin surrounding her. Only a little bit closer...

He stepped out of the car and the moment was gone. Madison followed, hoping her face wasn't broadcasting her thoughts from moments before.

"Where are we?" she asked, pleased that her voice sounded steady and solid. She looked around. Under normal circumstances, she would be close to panic at being in a situation like this – empty lot, unknown destination, accompanied by a man she'd known for only a week. But right now, the only trepidation she felt was for her heart.

"Washaway Beach." Dylan pointed towards a well-worn dirt path through the trees. "Right over this incline. Come on, let's check it out."

Just as he had the night before, Dylan reached out and laced his fingers through hers. Madison felt her heart speed up at the casualness of the gesture.

Determined to regain some semblance of balance, she cleared her throat and blurted out the first thing that came to her mind. "Why do they call it Washaway Beach?"

Dylan laughed and squeezed her hand. "Because that's exactly what it's doing—washing away." He swept his free hand in front of him in an expansive gesture. "If you look at photos or maps from decades ago, the beach was twice as far from the road as it is right now. The ocean has carved away the land."

"Amazing."

"That's one of the things I love about the coast—its unpredictability." He pointed to the north. "There used to be houses in that direction, but they washed away with the beach. So to keep other people from losing their homes, Westport took ownership of the land and is holding it in a public trust."

With a sinking sensation in her gut, Madison realized that

this was the very land Donovan coveted for their beachfront condominiums. "It must be pretty desirable property."

"We've had some pretty hefty offers, even though it would be the height of stupidity to build on land that's being reclaimed by the ocean a few feet every year. But I don't think the city will ever budge."

Unfortunately, Madison was afraid he was right. And now that she knew the reasoning behind the city's stubbornness, she found it hard to argue the point.

Well, she'd have plenty of time to worry about that later. They had arrived at Washaway.

Now that they had reached the end of the path, the trees ended and the beach took over, rolling waves of sand topped by fronds of beach grass bent double under the force of the wind. The roar of the waves, coupled with the wind, made conversation all but impossible.

They picked their way down to the waterline, standing far enough back to dodge the crashing waves. From solid ground, Madison could appreciate their beauty and power much more than she had on board *The Lucky Strike*. They stood together, gazing out at the rolling surf, turned steel gray by the dark clouds overhead.

Madison shivered and pulled her coat closer, warding off the icy reach of the blustery wind. Dylan must have noticed, because suddenly he was behind her, wrapping his arms around her and shielding her from the wind.

"It's beautiful out here, isn't it?" He spoke right in her ear, the warm puff of his breath sending delicious shivers down her spine. "This is one of my favorite spots in Westport." She felt the slight movement as he turned his head toward the surf once again.

She twisted slightly. "Then thank you for sharing it with me," she said, her lips almost touching the curve of his ear.

Dylan turned back, bending his neck so that their foreheads touched. His level gaze caught hers, and her eyes widened.

In the space of a breath, his lips touched hers, and the storm surrounding them faded to nothingness.

Chapter Six

His lips brushed against hers, feather-light, once, twice. Then he pulled back slightly, causing her heart to stop for a moment. But it was only to tilt his head to a better angle before claiming her mouth again.

Even in the chill wind Madison felt heat spiral through her body. This was a kiss to melt the polar ice caps, a kiss unlike any she'd ever experienced before. His lips were strong and firm, coaxing her to abandonment.

With a sigh, she turned in the circle of his embrace until they were face to face. She wrapped her arms around his neck and gave herself over to his kiss.

Her fingers tangled in his thick brown hair, urging him closer. He quickly complied, parting his lips as he deepened the kiss.

Even through the layers of clothing she could feel the taut muscles of his chest, his strong shoulders, the solid weight of his thighs. She moaned against his mouth, stunned by the sensations ricocheting through her. The cold air of the late-spring storm buffeted her, contradicting the bonfire sparking inside.

His hands burrowed under her jacket to pull her closer. He slid one hand down, beneath her sweater, to touch the bare skin of her back.

Both of them shuddered at the skin-to-skin contact. Taking her cue from Dylan, Madison pushed open his jacket and scrabbled at his shirt, pulling it out of the waistband of his jeans. She moved both hands from his waist up the smooth expanse of his back. Muscles bunched and flexed under her touch, sparking desire deep inside.

Suddenly Dylan pulled back, drawing in a shuddering breath, his forehead resting against hers. He withdrew his hands from under her clothing, leaving her oddly chilled. He looped his arms around her shoulders, anchoring her, sheltering her.

She pulled back as well, resting her arms around his waist, her heart beating triple time. She couldn't catch her breath.

He said something, but the wind snatched away his words, so Madison shook her head and leaned an ear closer. With his lips touching the shell of her ear, he said, "Let's get out of the cold, okay?"

Madison nodded, acutely aware of the chill in the air now that their kiss had ended. She grasped his outstretched hand and walked with him back to the car.

Oh, Lord.

What had he done?

Madison sat huddled in the passenger seat of his car, studiously avoiding eye contact. Even with the heater full-blast, she shivered from the effects of the cold outside.

At least that was what Dylan tried to tell himself.

But from time to time, when she thought he wasn't looking,

her trembling fingers would brush her lips. And he knew he was in trouble.

Madison appeared to be as affected by their kiss as he was. And that couldn't be a good thing.

He'd convinced himself it wouldn't mean anything–just a physical attraction, a brief kiss. A city girl like Madison would be blasé about something like that.

And he could be blasé, too. At least his ex-wife had taught him that.

But evidently he wasn't the best of students, because when their lips met, he found himself surfing down a monster wave of desire.

Dylan stared out the windshield, his lips thinning with tension. He'd practically mauled her out there. So much for a fun, relaxing visit to the beach.

"Are you okay?" His voice sounded unnaturally loud in the close confines of his sedan. Tempering it a little, he added, "Warm enough yet?"

Her hand flew to her mouth again, but she snatched it back to her lap almost immediately. Color flooded her cheeks. "I'm fine, thank you."

"Let's stop at the Seafood Shack for a bite before we head back, okay? PB and J just didn't cut it for lunch."

She smiled. "Let me guess—Carly picked the menu, too."

"Bingo."

At the mention of his daughter, some of the tension eased out of the atmosphere of the car. "She's adorable," Madison said.

"And bright," Dylan added.

"Of course," she replied. "You're not biased at all, either."

"Completely objective," he agreed.

The silence in the car this time was much more comfortable. Then Madison shifted in her seat. "Are you sure you want to go to the Seafood Shack?"

"Too much grease for you, huh?"

She shook her head. "I was just thinking, with Sallie's reaction to us eating together the other day, you might not want to bring the same...person along so soon."

Ah. Now the truth came out. She didn't want to be seen in public with him. He gritted his teeth against the surge of anger that welled up. He'd been right the first time.

He was only good enough for a fling.

He nodded tersely and flicked on the turn signal. "On second thought, I'm not that hungry right now. Let's just head back to The Inn."

Madison bit her lip. "If that's what you want."

They drove home in silence.

Hoo, boy.

Way to complicate everything, Madison.

Finally back in her cabin after a tension-filled, silent ride home, she tossed her coat on the bed and paced the small room. Stressed, confused, and pretty much overwhelmed with emotion, Madison fell back on her usual tactic for dealing with nerve-racking situations–ignore them and throw herself into work. She sat down at the little table and pulled her laptop out of its carry bag. Within minutes it was plugged in, powered up, and connected to the Internet.

Seventy-four messages? Since this morning? Madison clicked on her e-mail Inbox with a sense of doom hovering over her. Sure enough, fully half of them were from Lily, all titled 'Urgent'. She opened the last one, sent just a minute or two ago.

"Please, Madison, call me as soon as you get this message. I can't get through on your cell and you have to hear this from me first."

Oh God, oh God, oh God... Madison dug through her purse with shaking hands and pulled out her cell phone. A quick glance told her she'd turned it off at some point, probably on her way to the beach with Dylan. Yet another reason to stay far away from him—she would never leave her phone off during the day normally.

"Lily Winters," the familiar voice intoned.

"It's Maddie," she said, trying to keep calm. "What's going on?"

"Where have you been?" Lily hissed, as if trying to keep from being overheard. "I've been trying..."

"Yes, I know. My phone was off. Come on, Lily, you're scaring me here."

"Look, I can only take a minute. And if they knew I was telling you this, I'd be in serious trouble. So you can't let on that you know, all right?"

"Lily..."

"All right?" Even over the phone line Madison could tell Lily was gritting her teeth.

"Of course, Lily. You know that." Heart pounding, she clutched the phone like a life preserver.

"In a confidential meeting today, Bob said you hadn't been keeping the company apprised of your progress. He insinuated that you were either taking a free vacation on Donovan's dime, or you were failing spectacularly like all the others. The board is steamed, Maddie. You need to update them ASAP, or they won't wait until you're back to terminate your contract."

"They are not going to terminate my contract." Madison ground out each word, her neck muscles clenching like a fist.

"If Bob has his way, they will."

"He specifically told me not to bother him with details until

I had a contract in hand. 'Handle it yourself' were his exact words."

"Well that's playing right into his hands at the moment. My advice would be to fax something concrete over as soon as possible – and not to Bob. Or at least copy it to someone else on the board so he can't sit on it."

Madison sighed, pinching the bridge of her nose. "Thanks, Lily. I'll take it from here."

They exchanged goodbyes and Madison hung up, tossing the cell phone on top of her coat. She was sorely tempted to flop down on the bed next to it and have a nice little screaming fit.

Bob was sabotaging her. It shouldn't have been a surprise, really; he had been gunning for her since her first year on the job. But now that she was tucked away on the edge of nowhere, working on the most hopeless project Donovan Development could offer, he was ratcheting up the smear campaign.

She glanced at her computer; the rest of the e-mail could wait. She had only a few hours before the end of the workday, and she needed to have something concrete faxed to the entire board today.

Unfortunately, she didn't have anything concrete yet. She aimed a half-hearted kick at the box full of paperwork that was resting under the windowsill. Over a week in this town and she was no closer to signing on a development deal than she had been when she first arrived.

Madison dropped into the nearest chair, crossed her arms on the tabletop and rested her forehead against them. She knew she'd been working like crazy to get the background information necessary to push the deal through–but right now she had nothing to show for it.

And maybe, in a tiny way, Bob was right. Maybe she had

been enjoying herself just a little too much. It was time to get back in gear.

"Hello there. It's Madison, isn't it?"

Madison blinked, startled, as the woman behind the counter smiled at her. "Yes, but..."

"How did I know?" She nodded sagely. "Ronnie Edwards was in the other day and told me all about the pretty young lady staying at her place. She described you to a tee, my dear."

Blushing, Madison stammered a thank you and approached the counter of the tiny Westport police department-slash-mayor's office-slash-town hall.

"Now, what can I do for you?"

Madison smiled. "I have a few questions, but at the moment you have me at a disadvantage. You know my name, but I don't know yours."

"Oh, goodness gracious. How rude can I be? I'm Nancy Case." She held out a hand, taking Madison's hand in a firm grip. "You said you had questions?"

"Yes." Madison dug in her purse and pulled out her daytimer. "I was wondering when the next city council meeting was scheduled."

"Two weeks from yesterday," Nancy replied promptly.

Madison scribbled a quick notation in her calendar. "And how does one apply to be on the schedule to present?"

"Oh, it's very complicated." Nancy raised an eyebrow, her eyes twinkling. "You ask me, and I put your name on the schedule."

"Sounds difficult," Madison agreed with a smile. "Okay, Nancy, this is my official request. Could I be on the schedule for the next meeting?"

"Sure thing." Nancy punched a few buttons on her computer and squinted at the screen. "It'll be a long night, with this being the last meeting before the summer break. You don't mind sitting, do you?"

"No, of course not," Madison replied.

"Don't suppose you'd rather wait until September, would you? Docket's wide open then."

Madison shook her head emphatically. "Sorry, can't wait that long."

"Okie-dokie." Nancy tapped a few more keys. "You're scheduled. What topic?"

"I'd rather have more details taken care of before I get specific," Madison hedged. "Let's just call it a business proposal."

"Ooh, sounds interesting!" Nancy chuckled. "Maybe you'll shake up the meeting a little. I hate to be negative, but they do get a little boring. At least the council will have something to discuss besides dock reservations and what color to paint the observation tower."

Oh, they'd be talking all right. Madison shoved down her twinge of guilt and thanked Nancy for her time.

Once outside the unassuming building, Madison stood on the sidewalk and contemplated her next move. She should probably send an update to the board. But was that the best way to handle things?

Right now, a rushed email from her would be like broadcasting that she'd been warned about the discussion in today's meeting. It would probably appear desperate and not too effective. But how else could she take care of the image problem Bob had created?

"It can't be that bad," a low voice murmured in her ear. A voice that sent goosebumps shivering over her arms.

Madison jumped, shoving the meeting notice in her bag as

she turned. "Dylan," she said, a slight quaver to her voice. "What are you doing here?"

"We're just walking down the docks in search of ice cream," he said. "What about you?"

Belatedly, Madison realized that Carly was standing next to him, clinging to his hand and hopping up and down in her excitement.

"Ice cweam!" Carly tugged on his hand, leaning her full body weight towards the center of town. "Now!"

Dylan staggered after Carly as she muscled her way slowly down the sidewalk. "See you around," he said.

Madison winced inwardly. He was obviously still angry about Washaway Beach, although she couldn't for the life of her figure out what she'd done to offend him.

"Come wif us!" Carly had stopped her determined progress and was now standing in the middle of the sidewalk, pointing at Madison.

"Oh, I couldn't," Madison demurred, but Carly insisted.

"Pwease?"

Madison looked at Dylan, unable to find a reasonable excuse for the pleading toddler.

Dylan held her gaze for a moment, then shrugged. "You're welcome to join us if you don't have other plans."

Madison had plans, all right, but she couldn't resist. In moments, she was walking down the sidewalk with father and daughter, taking Carly's other hand and helping Dylan lift her over random mud puddles. The little girl's giggles echoed off the calm water of the harbor.

She was glad that Carly was there, to provide a buffer. As it was, she was so tightly strung at being close to Dylan again she was afraid she'd snap into little shards if he touched her.

Part of her wanted to run as far and as fast as she could. He had the potential to actually distract her from the job she'd been sent here to do, and that was not acceptable. She hadn't worked this hard to throw away everything for a crush.

But another part of her would die happy if she could experience one of those kisses once again.

She swallowed and kept walking, hoping that at some point she would figure out just what she wanted to do.

Once inside Breakers Ice Cream Shoppe, the three placed their orders and took a seat at the counter. Carly dug into her scoop of vanilla-with-sprinkles with gusto.

Dylan stuck a spoonful of Chocolate Decadence in his mouth, his eyes closing as he savored the rich flavor. Madison swallowed convulsively, her mouth suddenly dry as dirt. She bit into her cookie dough ice cream, wincing at the sharp cold against her teeth. At least it distracted her from gaping at Dylan.

Except for the chill formality of his initial conversation, there was nothing in his manner that even hinted at the kiss they'd shared earlier. Maybe it meant nothing to him. Maybe she was the only one still quivering from the sensations caused by his lips on hers, his hands on her skin.

She sighed, spooning up another bite of ice cream. Yet another reason why they were so unsuited for each other. Ironic, though, that it was the big-city girl who dissolved in a puddle of mush from one kiss.

"I owe you an apology." Dylan's voice was low, and Madison shivered from the impact.

"Apology?" She darted a look at Carly. Thankfully, the little girl was completely engrossed in her ice cream. "No, you don't owe me..."

Dylan held up a hand, forestalling her protest. "Yes, I do." He turned slightly, angling his body towards hers while subtly blocking Carly from the conversation. "My behavior was horrible this afternoon, and I'm sorry."

"Behavior?" Madison swallowed, a sour taste in her mouth.

He nodded, twirling his spoon in the rapidly melting dish of ice cream. "I shouldn't have, well, you know." He flicked a glance at her under thick lashes. "It won't happen again."

She nodded slowly. Wasn't she supposed to be happy about this? The decision was out of her hands now. One less distraction, more reason to focus on work.

For once, the thought of work didn't console her.

"Well, I hope we can put it behind us," he continued, a serious expression on his face. "I certainly want your stay at The Inn to be comfortable."

Of course. He was looking out for his mother. She knew all about that, didn't she?

Madison smiled tightly and retrieved her bag, slinging it over one shoulder. "Thank you," she said, although she wasn't sure if she meant it for the apology or the ice cream. "I should be going, though. I'll see you around. You too, Carly," she added, smoothing one hand over Carly's fluffy curls. "Enjoy your ice cream."

And with a nod, she turned and walked out of the ice cream parlor.

Chapter Seven

Dylan leaned on the porch rail of Madison's little cabin, tilting his head back to catch the warmth of the sunlight before the afternoon fog rolled in completely.

A busy morning out on the ocean had cleared his head a bit and he realized that he owed Madison an apology for his apology. In trying to smooth things over, he'd managed to offend her. And that wouldn't do.

The ice-cream incident had set his mind at ease about one thing – Madison wasn't ashamed to be seen in public with him. She really had been telling the truth about the Seafood Shack.

Unfortunately, that meant he had jumped to a very wrong conclusion at Washaway, and had taken it out on her.

He transferred his peace offering from one hand to the other. Madison was taking a really long time answering the door; maybe she had gone out for a walk or something. Or to the library for "research" again. That woman worked more during her vacation than most people did on the job.

Dylan knocked again. No answer. He turned to go, nodding at the couple walking by hand-in-hand.

"You're a few hours too late," the man said, slowing down to talk.

"Late?" Dylan glanced around, half-expecting Madison to pop up from around a bend in the path. "What do you mean, late?"

The woman shook her head. "She's gone. We thought maybe she'd checked out. She was packing her car this morning, oh, about nine-thirty. Haven't seen her since."

Dylan's heart dropped. She'd left?

That was sudden. Unless, God, he must have screwed up worse than he'd thought yesterday.

He stalked off towards the main house, thanking the couple tersely as he walked by. Maybe his mother could shed some light on the situation.

Unfortunately, she was in the dark as much as he was.

"Gone?" Ronnie stared at him, her mouth hanging open. She shut it with a snap. "She didn't say anything."

"So she didn't check out?" Dylan sank down into the overstuffed chair that faced his mother's desk. "Didn't settle her bill before she left?"

"No," Ronnie said. "She must be coming back."

"Not necessarily," he muttered. "She put a credit card on file when she checked in, right?"

"Of course."

"So she could call from wherever she went and settle her bill over the phone."

"Madison wouldn't do that," Ronnie said indignantly. "She wouldn't leave without saying goodbye."

Dylan eyed his mother with open skepticism. "Mom, you've known her just over a week. I know you adore the woman, but how do you know this isn't *exactly* what she'd do?"

"It just isn't," she retorted, crossing her arms over her chest. "She'll be back."

Dylan shrugged. "Whatever makes you happy."

Ronnie *harrumphed* at him and shuffled some paperwork. Then she stopped and gave him The Look.

He decided on the direct approach. "What?"

"What do you mean, what?"

"You've obviously got something on your mind. You might as well go ahead and say it."

"What's going on between you and Madison?"

He shrugged. "Nothing."

She arched an eyebrow. "You've never taken such an interest in the comings and goings of my clients before."

"Most of your clients check out before they leave."

"We don't know she's gone for good, and don't change the subject." She paused. "Carly told me she had ice cream with you two yesterday."

"Ice cream doesn't equal a relationship."

Of course, she pounced. "But there is some kind of a relationship, isn't there?"

He stood. "You're hallucinating if you think there's something going on between me and Madison. Were you even here during my marriage? The last thing I need is someone like Karen."

Ronnie bristled. "She is nothing like Karen."

"Come on, Mom. She's a total city girl, wrapped up in being the perfect career woman. She can't even relax on her vacation. Have you seen the piles of paperwork she has in her cabin?"

"No, I haven't," she answered quietly. "But I find it interesting that you have."

He didn't have a response to that.

"It's a shame that you keep insisting on painting her with

71

your Karen brush. Anyone else can see that they're nothing alike." She fixed him with The Look again. "Madison will be back, Dylan. I'm sure of it. Maybe you should take some time to decide how you really feel about that."

And this time, when she turned back to her paperwork, Dylan knew he was well and truly dismissed.

Madison rolled down the window, breathing in the crisp tang of ocean air. The tension that had been sitting on her shoulders all day finally dissipated with the cleansing breeze.

Her headlights punched through the fog that had rolled in during the evening. Lily had tried to convince her to spend the night in Seattle and drive back tomorrow, but all Madison could think about was getting back to Westport.

Funny how she'd spent a week here and already it felt more like home than the city where she'd lived since college. Certainly the thought of falling into bed in the cozy little cabin was more tempting than her stark, utilitarian apartment in Seattle.

She had stopped by her place for a moment, just long enough to grab a few sweatshirts and jeans to add to her "vacation" wardrobe. The resort-wear collection she'd originally packed for her month in Westport had been sadly inappropriate; more casual, warmer gear would be much appreciated.

For a brief moment she thought about making an obligatory call to her mother. Then she looked at her answering machine. The little red light glowed steadily.

Even though Madison had been gone for a week, her mom hadn't bothered to call. And neither had anyone else.

It was too depressing to think about, so she caught a quick bite with Lily and then headed back to the coast.

The day trip to Seattle had been spur of the moment, but a very good decision. The look on Bob's face when she walked into the office, binders in hand, had been well worth the drive. And with the information she'd delivered to the board, Madison had bought herself a little more breathing room.

Madison smiled, satisfied that she'd silenced her most vocal critic for the time being. Bless Lily for giving her a heads up.

The smile slid just a fraction. If she was being completely honest, she owed Dylan a debt of gratitude, too. His calm dismissal of their kiss yesterday had bothered her so much that she'd been unable to sleep. After a few hours of tossing and turning, she'd finally given up and dug into her paperwork. By morning, she had a packet of information prepared for the board, complete with charts, graphs, and supplemental hand-outs. A few hours on the road, a stop at the copy store down the street from Donovan's headquarters, and she was ready for action.

Now, though, she was ready for sleeping. An image of the cabin flickered through her mind, tempting her with a comfy bed, a snuggly duvet, and soft, goosedown pillows.

Suddenly a new image superimposed over the first. A tangle of dark-brown hair rested on the pillow next to hers. Very masculine, very naked shoulders were visible above the edge of the duvet, although the rest of his body was cocooned beneath the soft yellow covers. He turned slowly, his face becoming visible. Dark stubble dusted his strong jaw. His lips curved in a sexy smile as he caught her gaze, his own eyes shadowed by lids fringed in thick lashes...

Madison shook herself and turned up the radio. She was getting dangerously tired if she was fantasizing about a man who'd made it clear he wanted nothing to do with her! At least she was almost home and would soon be falling into bed.

Alone.

Steam billowed around Dylan's head and shoulders, disappearing into the fog-shrouded treetops overhead. He sank down a little further into the sultry water.

Most nights he liked to relax with a visit to the outdoor spa, but tonight it wasn't having the desired effect. Half an hour in the hot tub had soothed his muscles, but his mind had yet to slow down.

Dylan leaned over the edge of the spa and checked the volume on his child monitor. Carly was sleeping soundly; most nights it would take an earthquake to wake her once she fell asleep. He set the monitor aside and slid deeper into the steaming water, rolling his shoulders in an attempt to relax some more.

He didn't think he'd been unfair in his assessment of Madison. She was a workaholic, no doubt. Anyone around her for more than a few minutes could see that. And she was definitely a city girl. On the other hand, she didn't get snobbish about Westport like Karen had. In fact, she'd come across as friendly and unassuming at both restaurants they'd gone to together.

Okay, to be fair, her initial negative attitude had focused more on him than on the town as a whole. She assumed he was a playboy beach bum, and had treated him accordingly. Even though she'd begun to backpedal after getting to know him better, it still stung.

But why did it bother him? She was temporary, just passing through, like Karen and other city visitors like her. She could already be gone, if her disappearance today was any indication.

He scrubbed a hand through his steam-dampened hair. That was the crux of the issue. Madison was gone.

He could complain all he wanted about her workaholic ways and her city-girl snobbery, but just the thought of her leaving–and not saying goodbye–was enough to send him into a funk.

Maybe it was the sweetness he saw in her smile. Maybe it was the gentle way she treated Carly, even when the toddler gave new definition to the phrase "terrible twos". Maybe it was the delight she took in experiencing Westport's attractions–fishing trips excepted, of course.

Maybe it was the fire singing through his veins at the thought of kissing her again.

Maybe he was just as guilty of assuming the worst as she was. But which was the real Madison? The workaholic snob, or the nice girl?

Dylan ducked under the steaming hot water, blowing out a burst of air in frustration. He should be thinking about the charter business, or his off-season work, or the city council meeting coming up in less than two weeks. The last thing he needed to have on his mind was a frustrating, appealing, confusing, *missing* woman like Madison.

The porch light was on. It hadn't been when she'd left, but then there was really no reason to leave the light on in broad daylight.

Back home in Seattle, if a light were on that she hadn't turned on herself, it would be reason to hightail it to the nearest police station. But here, Madison felt only a warmth spreading through her chest at the sight.

Even though she hadn't informed anyone that she was going, someone had taken the time to make her cabin a little more inviting, just in case she arrived after dark.

Madison blinked back the moisture that had gathered on her eyelashes. She must be more tired than she thought.

At the top of the steps she dropped her bags and fumbled in her purse for the key. She pushed the door open, pausing when a little "thud" drew her attention downward.

A small package lay tumbled over the doorframe. Someone had obviously leaned it up against the door, where it had gone unnoticed until the door opened and it fell inside. Madison picked it up and turned it over; it was nicely wrapped but no card was attached.

Intensely curious, she pulled her bags in and left them scattered on the floor in front of the kitchen table. Crossing the room, she switched on the bedside lamp and settled down on top of the comforter. As much as her fingers were itching to tear into the paper, years of training won out. She slid a finger under the tape, loosened it, and unfolded the paper neatly. The item inside slipped quietly into her waiting hands.

It was fabric. A stretchy, shiny fabric, and not very much of it. Madison frowned, shaking it out to get a better look.

Suddenly, she realized what it was, and dropped it to the bedspread with a little yelp.

It was a swimsuit. A brilliant, jewel-tone blue, with strands of silver threaded throughout, it was a rather modest one-piece, but Madison blushed furiously nonetheless. A swimsuit!

She lifted the packaging and shook it, but nothing else dropped out. There was no note, but Madison knew who had left it on her doorstep anyway.

The question was, what exactly did Dylan mean by giving her such a personal—*intimate*—gift?

And what in the world was she going to do about it?

Technically, Madison's cabin wasn't on the way from the hot

tub to the main house. But somehow Dylan found himself wandering past the little yellow building post-soak anyway.

Her porch light was on, which wasn't a surprise. He'd turned it on himself after dinner, first suffering through a lecture from his mother about honoring the privacy of their guests. It must have stuck, though, because despite the temptation to snoop around, he merely unlocked the door, slid a hand in to flip the light switch, and locked the door again.

A closer look told him the package was gone. That was a positive development. There was a ninety-nine percent chance that Madison had the suit in her hot little hands, since porch theft was pretty much unheard of in Westport.

For a moment, he had a pang of doubt about his gift. Maybe she'd read more into it than he intended. But, damn it, the hot tub was one of The Inn's featured attractions. And if she was too busy to pick up a suit, he was more than happy to do it for her.

And if by chance she ended up sharing the hot tub with him one night before her sabbatical was up, he wouldn't complain, either.

So he wasn't being totally altruistic. At this point, he really didn't care.

He peered at the curtained window. A faint light glowed from within. She was back for certain, then.

The tension that had slowly dissipated with the soak in the tub came roaring back with a vengeance. And behind that tension was a relief that he wasn't willing to explore just now. Before he was quite aware of what he was doing, Dylan had charged up the steps two at a time.

He pounded on the closed door with his fist. The door swung open to reveal a sleepy-eyed Madison, outfitted in flannel pajamas in a clouds-on-blue-sky print.

Without thinking, he reached out and grasped her by the

shoulders, hauling her in for a kiss. Her little gasp of surprise was quickly swallowed up, the kiss immediately spiraling out of control. After a moment or two of indecision, she wrapped her arms around his neck and kissed him back. Her full breasts flattened against his chest through the soft flannel of her pajama top. His hands slid down her back to cup the curve of her ass. She moaned into his mouth.

Abruptly, he broke the kiss, setting her back until he was holding her at arms' length. Chest heaving, heart pounding triple-time, he glared at her. "Where the hell have you been?"

Chapter Eight

Madison stared. She blinked twice, trying to clear the muzziness from her head. Nope, Dylan was still there, hands on her shoulders, glaring at her in the dim glow of the porch light.

Her lips felt puffy. She couldn't catch her breath. He'd just grabbed her and kissed her. And then yelled at her.

What the hell was going on?

"Nice to see you, too," she said, stepping back so she could cross her arms over her chest. She didn't want there to be any chance he could tell that her nipples were tight and aching beneath her flannel jammies.

Oh, God. She was wearing her flannel jammies.

Should she go change? Throw on a bathrobe? It was clear across the room, and she really didn't want to draw attention to herself by scurrying all the way over to fetch it.

She eyed Dylan. Compared to his swim trunks and towel ensemble, she was practically wearing a nun's habit.

But she didn't think Dylan would kiss a nun with quite that much enthusiasm.

"Well?" He glowered at her, obviously irritated.

"Well, what?"

Dylan blew out a quick, annoyed breath. "Where in the world have you been? I've—we've—been worried sick."

It was a small slip, but a slip nonetheless. Madison bit back a smile. "I didn't realize I needed permission to leave campus, sir."

More glowering. He obviously wasn't in a mood to joke.

"I just got back from Seattle," she said, hoping he wouldn't expect more details.

If anything, the scowl on his face grew deeper. "You went to Seattle for the day."

"I do live there," Madison said, finally giving in and stomping across the room to grab her robe.

Of course, he followed. And stood there, waiting for more information.

Shoving one arm into the sleeve of her robe, she continued, "I had to check my messages, get some clothes, air out the apartment, stop by work..."

"Aha!" he shouted, stabbing his finger into the air like a detective in a junior high murder mystery production. "I knew it! I knew you couldn't stay away from work!"

And though it was the absolute truth, part of Madison wilted at the smug look on Dylan's face.

"I'm on sabbatical, Dylan," she said, tying her robe with a little more force than absolutely necessary. "Not unemployed. I still have responsibilities I can't ignore."

The triumph slowly leached out of Dylan's expression, leaving him looking tired and sad. "I know."

Madison nodded, biting her lip. She looked around, as if hoping a conversational topic would leap out at her from the tidy room. She opened her mouth, hoping something half-coherent would tumble out, but Dylan beat her to it.

"Sorry I bit your head off," he mumbled, running a hand through his still-damp hair. "It's just that you were gone all day, with no word, and..."

Madison laughed softly, touched and amused that he actually had been worried about her. Used to being the steady, responsible one, she couldn't think of a time in the past ten years that anyone had been concerned about her, and it was a novel experience.

Dylan drew himself up, eyes narrowed. "I should go," he said, turning towards the half-open door.

On impulse, Madison reached out and touched his bare shoulder, ignoring the jolt of desire that raced through her at the contact with his heated skin. "I'm sorry," she said. "Would you like a cup of tea? Some cookies? Maybe a t-shirt?"

Dylan glanced down at his bare chest, his upper body covered only by the towel looped around his shoulders. "I probably should have changed before dropping by, but I was just on my way back from the hot tub and saw that your light was on."

"No, that's fine." Madison sat down in the opposite chair. An awkward silence fell.

Dylan cleared his throat. "Maybe next time you could join me." A wicked smile played over the corners of his lips. "Seeing as you no longer have the bathing suit excuse."

"So that *was* from you," Madison said, her cheeks heating with embarrassment.

"Who else? My mother? Customer service at The Inn is excellent, but I don't think she'd buy you a swimsuit unless you asked."

"I—I can't accept it."

Dylan's eyebrows drew together. "Why on earth not?"

She gestured helplessly with one hand. "It's just so—personal."

With a deft movement, he caught her fluttering hand with his own. "True."

"But we don't—we haven't—"

"Haven't we?" He smiled, running one finger across her knuckles.

She shivered at the contact. "I don't know what to say."

"Don't say anything." He squeezed her hand lightly. "Just try it on."

"Now?" She glanced at him, momentarily captured by the heated promise in his eyes. Did she really sway towards him, or was the movement a product of her overactive imagination?

"No better time than the present."

She looked at the package again, tempted. "But I'm not sure..."

"Consider it being a good hostess." At her blank look, he added, "Making sure your guest doesn't feel underdressed."

Despite the heat crawling up her neck at the reminder, she laughed. "All right. Wait here."

Dylan sat back in his chair, lacing his fingers together behind his head. "Oh, believe me. I'm not going anywhere."

She grabbed the package and headed into the bathroom, closing the door tightly behind her. Then she clutched the edge of the sink and held on for dear life.

What the hell was she doing? Was she actually going to strip down to a swimsuit and model it for a man she hardly knew?

Taking a deep breath, she pulled the suit out of the wrapping paper and shook it out. Apparently the answer was yes.

Before she could talk herself out of it, she was shimmying into the royal blue swimsuit, her flannel jammies discarded on the bathroom floor.

Taking a deep breath, she ran her hands through her hair.

Yeah, this was out of character for her. But here, in a town on the backside of beyond, around people she'd likely never see again after this month was up, she could act a little out of the ordinary. Do as Lily kept pestering her to do and have a vacation fling.

And truth was, despite what she'd told Dylan when they first met, she was more than interested.

She was ready to take a chance.

With a last look at the mirror, she reached for the doorknob. Then, because she wasn't quite that daring, she grabbed her robe and slid it on, belting it around her waist.

Dylan glanced up as she slipped out of the bathroom, a smile toying at the corners of his mouth. "That doesn't look like a bathing suit to me."

"I didn't want to be too predictable," she said, holding the lapel of the bathrobe closed. Her legs were bare beneath the robe.

"Hardly." He stood and pushed the chair in. "So are you planning to lose the robe, or just tease me with a peek a boo view?"

"I haven't decided," she said.

"Or maybe I get to decide," he said softly, reaching out and tracing one finger down the vee of her bathrobe. He hooked it in the overlap of terry fabric, brushing dangerously close to the swell of her breasts. He gently tugged her forward until she stood toe to toe with him.

He clamped down on the surge of desire that raced through him, urging him to rip off the bathrobe and explore the curves hidden beneath. Ever since their kiss on the beach he'd been obsessing about the soft skin he'd stroked beneath her sweater, the gentle indent of her waist he could almost span with his hands. He wanted to see her, touch her again.

But it had to be her step. He'd handed her the challenge—the ball was in her court now.

Her eyes, wide and unblinking, focused on his face. Her breathing was shallow and rapid, her pulse beating a mile a minute at the base of her throat. It was clear she was as turned on as he was.

The question was, what was she going to do about it?

A few days ago he would have assumed he knew the answer. She was from the city, with a high-powered career and most likely a social life to match. Of course she'd be the type to reach out and take what she wanted.

But despite her fears to the contrary, she was the furthest thing from predictable he could imagine.

Instead of a man-eater, Madison was almost—shy. More inclined to cover up than flaunt her figure. Even now, she stood in front of him, her expression a mix of desire and trepidation. Even now, she hesitated.

Regretfully, he slid his hand away from her robe and stepped back. The last thing he wanted was to push her in a direction she wasn't ready to go.

"Wait." Glancing down, Madison pulled at the tie of her robe. The sides of the fabric parted, revealing a glimpse of bare leg.

"Are you sure?"

She nodded. Then, taking a deep breath, she slipped the robe off her shoulders and let it drop to the floor.

Hot damn. Dylan was thankful that he was wearing board shorts, because anything tighter would have given away his physical response immediately.

As it was, she'd still be able to tell how hard he was for her if she so much as glanced that direction.

Shifting slightly, he ignored his throbbing cock and looked his fill.

He'd called it on the swimsuit, if he did say so himself. The dark blue fabric contrasted with her pale skin, and the silver accents brought a sparkle to her eyes. Or maybe it was the heat in her gaze that brightened them.

She colored slightly under his frank appraisal, and the tip of her pink tongue darted out to moisten her lower lip.

It was all Dylan could do not to groan.

Lifting one shoulder, she said softly, "Well?"

He cleared his throat. "You look amazing."

She smiled and looked away. Then she bent down to pick up the robe.

He stopped her with a hand on her arm. The touch of skin on skin made them both suck in a breath. "Don't."

"But I—"

"Let's go down to the hot tub," he said.

"I shouldn't." She shook her head, soft blonde hair brushing her bare shoulders. "Besides, you've already been in the hot tub tonight."

"So?" He rolled his eyes. "No rule that you can't use the hot tub more than once in a 24 hour period. Besides, it seems a shame to waste the opportunity."

She bit her lip, which made him harden even more. "I don't know..."

"Come on," he cajoled, slipping his hand down her arm to lace his fingers with hers. "What's the fun of having a new swimsuit if you don't go try it out?"

She glanced over at her briefcase. Then, squaring her shoulders, she turned back to him. "You're right. Let's do it."

Let's do it? Madison dug around in the bottom of her suitcase, teeth clenched. Was that really the best she could do? Finally snagging her flip-flops, she zipped up the case and sat down on the bed to put them on.

She couldn't come up with something sexy and seductive to say? Might as well slap a big "L"-for-loser on her forehead.

"Ready?" Dylan stood next to the door, an extra towel in his hand. The smoldering look he gave her was enough to make her thighs quiver. Which wasn't necessarily a good thing when wearing a high-cut bathing suit and nothing else.

She grabbed her robe and pulled it on. "Ready."

And she was. Crazy as it seemed, and as out of character, she was ready to follow Lily's advice and have a holiday fling. And she couldn't think of anyone she'd want to share it with more than Dylan.

He had a life here in Westport. She'd be gone in a less than three weeks now. It was perfect for a short-term affair, which was all she could fit into her life right now.

With a smile, she took the towel from him and opened the door. The cool night air wrapped around her bare legs, sending a shiver down her spine.

Or maybe it was the man next to her, so warm and solid and male, making her shake with desire.

He took the key from her and locked the door behind them, then tucked it in the pocket of her robe. He laced his fingers with hers and set off down the path to the hot tub, his thumb tracing patterns on the back of her hand.

"So how's Carly?" She couldn't think of anything else to say, especially when all her attention was focused on the slight callous of his hand against her palm. And then she hoped with all her might that the mention of his two year old wouldn't be a complete mood killer.

"Fine," Dylan said, a brief smile flashing across his face. "Sleeping like a baby."

"I guess your mother is watching her," she said.

"She's in the house, but I'm keeping an ear out." He patted a square piece of plastic clipped to the band of his swimsuit. "Wide-range baby monitor. If she whimpers, I hear it. That way I can use the hot tub or take a walk without worrying too much—or dropping it all in my mom's lap."

"That's sweet."

"Thanks," he said. "I think."

"Sweet is good." She squeezed his hand. "Very good."

"Well, then." He grinned down at her, his teeth gleaming in the darkness. "Good to know."

Their footsteps crunched on the pathway as they wound their way through the woods to the hot tub. Finally, they turned the curve and saw the steam rising.

Thankfully, it was empty. Madison wasn't sure what she would have done if there'd been anyone else in the hot tub.

They left their towels and other items on the edge of the tub, and slipped into the bubbling water.

Madison sighed as the heat wrapped around her, soothing the tension that had settled in her shoulders. "Wow," she breathed.

"I know," Dylan said. Then they soaked in silence for a while, the sound of the wind ruffling the treetops mingling with the low hum of the hot tub motor. Every once in a while, Madison's foot would bump Dylan's, or their knees would touch.

She was almost trembling, she wanted him so much.

"So was your trip to Seattle a success?" Dylan's voice echoed in the clearing. "Did you accomplish everything you wanted to?"

He wanted to talk? Now?

"Fine," she said. She really, really didn't want to talk about work right now. Then she changed the subject. "How was fishing today?"

"Great." He grinned at her, a glint in his eye. "You could try it again, you know. Free trip on the house."

"No, thank you." She barely suppressed a shudder. "Definitely not my cup of tea. But you must like it. I suppose you really have to love fishing to be a charter boat captain."

"Well, that helps," Dylan replied, the glint of humor in his eyes indicating that her quiver of distaste hadn't gone unnoticed. "And I do. I love being on the ocean." He smiled, his gaze slipping involuntarily to the edge of the clearing and the rumbling, invisible ocean beyond.

"You're lucky that you have your mom to help out with Carly while you're on the boat," she said.

He nodded. "I owe her a lot."

"She loves being a grandma," Madison said. "I'm sure she doesn't mind watching Carly."

"Yes, I know," Dylan said, "But she does enough already. When I became a father, I knew I needed to take responsibility for Carly, not pawn her off on other people. Especially after her mother took off. I want to raise my daughter, be a real dad. I never want to be an absentee parent."

"Well, you're doing a great job," she said softly.

"Yeah, well." He shrugged. "I do my best. Most of the year it's easy. I spend seven months out of the year being a full-time dad. It's just the summer that's crazy."

"You only run the charter boat five months a year?"

Dylan smiled. "Only when the fish are running and the government says it's legal."

"Wow." Madison sipped at her tea. "You must make a ton of money at it."

At that, Dylan let out a soft bark of laughter. "Not even

close," he said. "Barely enough to keep *The Lucky Strike* afloat and my deckhand paid."

"Then how do you make a living?"

"My other job."

Madison blinked at him. "You have another job?"

"In the off-season." Dylan stretched his arm across the back of the hot tub, curling his fingers around her shoulder. "I'm a freelance web designer."

"You have got to be kidding me!" Madison sat up, sloshing water over the edge of the hot tub.

"Why? Because I'm just a resort-town slacker?"

Madison could feel the blush heating her face, appalled at hearing her initial attitude tossed back at her. But a closer look at Dylan's face revealed a sly smile, completely without rancor.

"I'm just giving you a hard time," he said. "You had no reason to know about my other job."

Madison nodded once, quickly, letting her hair tumble down and obscure her face. God, what he must think of her...

Dylan waved a hand as if to dismiss the topic. "Anyway, it's a perfect job for me since I can pretty much set my own work schedule. I take a sabbatical during the fishing season and work the rest of the year. Mostly evenings and naptime, so Carly can come first. Plus, I can put my degree to good use."

Madison was almost afraid to ask. "Your degree?"

"I have a Master's in computer science from the University of Washington."

She leaned forward and rested her head against his shoulder. "I am such an idiot..." she mumbled.

"Hey, don't worry about it." He rested his hand on her neck, holding her close. "How could you have known?"

Her skin shivered with a million goosebumps. "I should never have assumed..."

His fingers started to move, stroking the exposed skin at the base of her neck. "You're not the only one who jumped to conclusions, you know."

"But I–" She raised her head, staring into Dylan's eyes with anguish.

He shook his head, slowly, a soft smile playing on his lips. Then he increased the pressure on the back of her head, pulling her inexorably forward.

He kissed her cheek, softly, and she let out a breath she hadn't even realized she was holding. Dylan tilted his head slightly and, finally, covered her lips with his own.

Sensation exploded along every nerve ending, sending tremors down Madison's arms. She leaned into the kiss, opening her mouth to his, wanting this contact. Wanting so much more.

Her arms came up around his neck and pulled him closer. He smiled against her mouth and adjusted his embrace, lifting her into his lap. Madison gasped at the intimate contact, but the soft sound was swallowed by his kiss.

His swim trunks were only a thin barrier, her swimsuit not much more. Heated desire spiraled through her, causing her breath to hitch and her pulse to race.

Sensations she couldn't even name ricocheted through her body, sending her into sensory overload.

He slid a finger under the strap of her bathing suit and pulled it down, then repeated the action with the other strap. She moaned against his mouth as he cupped one breast, circling her nipple with a calloused thumb.

Her legs were wrapped around his waist, the heavy thickness of his erection nudging against her. She arched her back, eyes squeezed shut, as Dylan slowly kissed his way down her neck, across her collarbone, and took one taut nipple into his mouth.

Heat spiraled through her, pulsing between her thighs, as he tormented her with teasing little strokes of his tongue. One hand splayed through the damp curls at the base of his neck, the other grasping the edge of the hot tub.

Her breath was coming in short gasps when she gradually became aware that Dylan had stopped. Madison opened her eyes and met his gaze. "What?"

"Nothing," he said, planting a quick hard kiss full on her lips. "It's just that if we don't cool things off now, it'll be hard to stop. And it's not impossible that other guests of The Inn might stop by for a late night dip."

He slipped her bathing suit back on, adjusting the straps so it fit right.

She leaned forward, resting her forehead against his, then kissed his temple before sliding off his lap to sit beside him.

Every molecule of her body was aching for him. Frustrated desire swamped all rational thought, though on some level she was grateful that he'd been coherent enough to put on the brakes.

She'd been half naked in a public location. Who was she, and what had she done with Madison McIntyre?

And was there a chance the new, risk-taking Madison might stick around for a little while?

The silence stretched between them until Madison latched on to the first conversational topic she could scrounge up in her overheated brain. "Do you remember your first time on a boat?"

Dylan turned back, his attention once again focused on her. "Oh, yeah. I was nine the first time my dad took me out on the *Lucky Strike*."

Madison fought to keep her jaw from dropping. In her book, that was tantamount to child abuse! "Hmm," she murmured noncommittally.

Some of her horror must have been evident, though, because Dylan took one look at her face and laughed out loud. "It's obvious you're not from around here," he teased. "Nine is ancient when it comes to taking your first ride on a fishing boat."

"Practically a senior citizen," she said gravely, hiding a smile.

"Well, in the cutthroat world of elementary school, that's true," Dylan said. "I was so relieved when Mom gave in the summer before fourth grade. Finally shut Tim Gellert up."

Madison glanced up sharply, but saw only wry humor on Dylan's face. "Class bully?"

"Best friend," he replied, one finger tracing the whorl of her ear. He couldn't seem to stop touching her, and she, of course, had no desire to complain. "Always in competition with each other, though. His dad took him out when he was eight, and he lorded it over me for an entire year."

"What's he doing now?"

Dylan glanced out toward the hidden shore again. "Tim died in a fishing accident four years ago."

"I'm so sorry," Madison said, placing her hand on his.

Dylan turned his hand over slowly, until they were palm to palm. "Tim was commercial fishing in Alaska over the winter," he said quietly. "Lots of guys do it, especially the ones who don't have an off-season job waiting for them. The money is great, but you're away from home for months at a time, and it's incredibly dangerous. His boat went down in a storm and the entire crew was lost."

"Oh, Dylan..." Madison squeezed his hand tightly. He gripped it for a moment, then pulled his hand away. Her hand felt cold at the loss of contact.

"Fact of life in a fishing town," he said with a shrug. "I think

Mom and I counted over forty people we know who've died young, mostly drownings. You get really used to funerals."

"How horrible!" Madison crossed her arms, tucking her hands under her elbows for warmth as a cold chill traveled down her spine. "How can you work in such a dangerous job? What about Carly?"

At the mention of his daughter's name, Dylan's face lost all traces of warmth. "What about her?"

Madison ignored the warning note in his voice and plowed on, her stomach churning at the thought of another child left fatherless by unnecessary risks. "How can you go out on that boat every day, risking your life, when you have a defenseless child at home who depends on you? You said yourself that you don't need it to make a living. I can't believe you'd be so irresponsible!"

Silence stretched between them. The hot tub motor cycled on, startlingly loud in the charged atmosphere. She watched as a muscle worked in Dylan's jaw.

"I don't recall that my daughter's well-being is any of your business," he said tightly.

"Maybe it's not, but it sure should be yours," she retorted, too angry and worried to modify her reaction. The person who took the risks never seemed to pay the price; it was the ones left behind who suffered.

Dylan stood and retrieved his towel, wrapping it around his waist with sharp, barely controlled movements. He didn't look at her. "I think this conversation is over," he said, stepping out of the tub. "I'll walk you home."

"Dylan..."

He stood at the bottom of the steps, waiting for her. She bit her lip and climbed out, retrieving her towel and bathrobe. Tying the robe around her waist, she slipped on her flip flops.

They walked back to The Inn in silence, Dylan's anger a palpable force between them. On the deck of her cabin, he stepped aside and waited as she unlocked the door.

And with a narrow-eyed glance, Dylan said goodnight and walked away as Madison shut the door quietly behind him.

Chapter Nine

"I see Madison got back last night," Ronnie remarked off-handedly as she handed Dylan his travel mug of coffee.

He mumbled angrily, setting the mug aside to shrug into his raingear. The weather report had been grim, with storms predicted for later in the day, but so far the wind was light enough to allow the boats to go out.

"But I guess you already knew that," she continued, cheerfully ignoring his warning glare.

Dylan reached behind the counter to grab his boots. He sat heavily in the kitchen chair and tugged them on, resolutely avoiding his mother's curious gaze.

"And her trip yesterday took less time than you expected," she said, sliding a tray of scones into the waiting oven.

"Drop it," he growled. Slapping a baseball cap on his head, he stood to go.

A hesitant knock at the door stopped him. When he didn't act immediately to answer, Ronnie scooted around him and pulled the door open.

Madison stood on the doorstep, hands twisting the hem of her cream-colored cable knit sweater. She looked uncertainly from Ronnie to Dylan. "May I come in?" she asked in a low voice.

Dylan shrugged and turned away. Ronnie rolled her eyes and placed an arm around Madison's shoulder, steering her around Dylan and seating her at the kitchen table. "Can I get you a cup of coffee, dear?"

Madison shook her head. "No, thanks. I'm fine."

But she wasn't. It was evident in the bruised-looking shadows beneath her eyes and the tension in her jaw. Despite his bone-deep anger, Dylan felt himself softening towards her.

With a muttered curse, he set his mug down on the counter, grateful for the spill-proof lid as the hot liquid sloshed around inside. "Mom, don't you have work to do?"

"Actually, I..." her voice trailed off as she caught sight of his face. "Yes, I—need to fold the linens. Excuse me." With a sympathetic look at both of them, she slipped out of the room.

"Morning." He wasn't quite willing to call it a good morning, but he could concede the actual time of day.

"Morning," she replied, her glance darting around the cheerful kitchen.

At least they agreed on one thing, Dylan thought wryly. Even if it was the only thing they'd ever see eye to eye on. He pushed the depressing thought away and focused on Madison.

Her face was paler than usual, which he wouldn't have thought possible. Thin lines etched the sides of her mouth and the outside corners of her eyes. She looked as tired and worn out as he felt.

Well, good. It would have been completely unfair if he were the only one who'd spent a restless night last night.

"Look, Dylan, I..." she stopped, finally looking him in the

eye for the first time since appearing on his doorstep. "I owe you an apology. A big one. And I couldn't let you leave today without telling you so."

"Okay," he said cautiously. He was willing to listen, but he'd be damned if he made it any easier for her.

"The thing is," she said, twisting at her sweater again. She took a deep breath and started over. "The thing is, I had no right to say what I did last night. I was wrong, and I apologize."

He just nodded, not quite trusting himself to speak.

"For what it's worth, I think you're a wonderful father, no matter what you do for a living," she added.

"Apology accepted," he said, taking a sip of his coffee.

Her eyes still had a wounded look to them, as if she was the injured party. What, did she expect him to fall at her feet and thank her for apologizing?

Deep down, he knew he wasn't being very gracious, but beneath his anger was another emotion he'd spent the night ruthlessly suppressing. Much as he hated to admit it, he was hurt.

In any case, he didn't have time to deal with it right now.

Dylan glanced at his watch. Madison caught the movement and pushed back in her chair. "You're late."

"Yes," he said, tugging the cap down a little further.

Madison sighed, her gaze slipping away to the corner of the kitchen. "Sorry I kept you."

"It's okay."

"Will you have time to talk—later?" She twisted the hem of her sweater again. It wouldn't be good for much besides the rag pile once she got done with it.

He hesitated, not sure he wanted to get into such a sore subject with Madison again.

She caught the expression on his face and hastened to

explain. "I owe you more than just an apology, Dylan. I owe you an explanation. But it'll take longer than you have right now."

He relented, trying not to care about the expression of relief on her face as he nodded.

He stood to go, wishing he could forget how her comments had wounded him last night. They weren't vicious, but the heartfelt emotion behind them had ripped at his gut.

It was clear that the danger inherent in his job pushed some button for her; maybe when they talked tonight he'd understand her position more.

But right now, he wasn't sure he wanted to.

The sun was well into its downward descent when Madison finally looked up from her paperwork. Even through the lacy curtains she could that see the afternoon was shaping up beautifully.

Hurriedly putting away her work, Madison shrugged into a butter yellow cardigan and stepped out the door of her cabin.

Once on the crushed-rock path, however, her pace slowed. Although she'd apologized to Dylan this morning–way, way too early this morning—things were still rough between them. And she certainly wasn't looking forward to explaining her behavior of the night before.

A shiver traveled down her spine and back again. Right now, everything in her life seemed to be spinning out of control–her job, her personal life, her emotions. She could hardly wait to finish the Westport job and get back to her safe, predictable, manageable life.

Madison shook off the nagging little voice that added "boring" and "lonely" to that list and began walking towards the main house. Time to get her full apology over with.

But as she neared the front porch, the door opened and Dylan walked through, holding hands with little Carly. She was bundled up in a thick windbreaker and bright yellow boots, and she clutched a bucket and shovel in her free hand.

"Beach!" Carly crowed, catching sight of Madison. She tugged free of her father's hand and ran down the steps, stopping in front of Madison with a wide grin on her face. "You, too," she wheedled.

Madison looked from daughter to father, almost glad to have an excuse to postpone her conversation with Dylan. "Thanks, sweetie, but I don't want to interfere with your Daddy time."

Dylan snorted. "Where Carly is concerned, the more people at the beach, the better. A wider audience to appreciate her sand castles." He joined them on the walkway. "You're welcome to come along."

Madison looked him in the eye. So much for a reprieve. No, this was no time to be chicken—she had to follow through. "Sounds great," she said. "Are we walking or driving?"

Carly took off down the crushed rock path as fast as her chubby legs could carry her. "Dis way!"

With a good-natured grin, Dylan walked briskly after her, motioning for Madison to catch up. She looked down at her outfit, shrugged, and hurried down the path.

Once at Dylan's side, Madison slowed her pace a bit. The two of them walked a few steps behind Carly, who was swinging her bucket and singing loudly at the top of her lungs.

Madison turned to Dylan. "I'm afraid I don't know much about kid's entertainment these days. What is she singing?"

Dylan smiled. "I have no idea. I'm pretty sure she's making it up as she goes along."

They walked along the path, heading deeper into the woods that ringed the property where The Inn stood. A low rumble caught Madison's ear. "I didn't realize we were so close," she said, belatedly recognizing the sound of the surf.

"Hard to get away from it in Westport," Dylan replied, holding aside a low-slung branch for Madison. "But yeah, beach access is one of the benefits of The Inn. Which you would have known if you'd taken a look at our website," he teased.

"I'm sure Lily noticed," Madison protested. "She said the website was..." Her voice trailed off. "You're the hotshot local web designer." She stopped in the middle of the path, hands on her hips. "I can't believe that you let me blather on about how great Lily said the site was without telling me you designed it!"

Dylan shot a glance at Carly, who was crouched in the middle of the path watching a caterpillar cross in front of her. He turned to Madison, placing a conciliatory hand on her shoulder. "You weren't blathering. It was just nice to get an honest compliment. And I did appreciate it."

Madison sucked in a breath. The sparks that flew when they touched would be a fire hazard on the dampest of days.

Dylan dropped his hand from her shoulder and turned to follow Carly once again.

Over a low rise, the woods shifted to packed sand and beach grass, and Carly churned her way over the dunes to the beach. Dylan, while never more than a few steps away, gave her enough space to explore. She dropped down on a wide expanse of sand well set back from the water's edge and began to dig.

As if by silent agreement, Dylan and Madison sat down on a large piece of driftwood between Carly and the ocean. A breeze ruffled the clumps of beach grass, and Madison pulled her sweater a little tighter.

"Cold?" Without waiting for a reply, Dylan slipped out of

his jeans jacket and wrapped it around her shoulders. His unique scent, spicy and masculine, rose from the well-worn fabric, while the residual heat of his body warmed Madison clear to her toes.

"Thanks," she said, flashing him a quick glance. Clearing her throat, Madison began, "About last night..."

Dylan cut her off. "You don't owe me an explanation," he said.

"Yes, I do."

Dylan shifted on the driftwood log, moving sideways so he was looking directly at her. Madison looked away, staring at the hardpack sand beneath her feet.

"When I was nine, my father died." She swallowed. Even after all these years, it was still hard to say.

Dylan touched her shoulder, caressing it gently in a wordless display of sympathy. The gesture was both comforting and disconcerting, as Madison fought to keep her emotions under control.

"He was a pilot." She flashed a wry smile at the sand. "Flying was his first, last and only love."

"What sort of flying?" Dylan's voice was low and soothing.

Her glance flickered upwards, subconsciously looking for clear skies. "Small planes mostly, although at one point he looked into getting a commercial pilot's license."

"What changed his mind?"

"My mother." Madison bit her lip. "Said it was too dangerous. I think what she really wanted was for him to get a practical job, something safer and more stable. But he wouldn't give it up. He took people up on air tours, gave flying lessons when he had the opportunity. And every chance he got, he was out at the airfield, tinkering with his plane. He even built it himself, from a kit. Called it his firstborn."

She looked up again, squinting in the late-afternoon

sunlight. "I used to beg him to take me along, but I was 'too young'. Besides, my mother would have pitched a royal fit if he'd even let me polish a wing or whatever you do with a plane. It was too dangerous for a little girl. And I guess she was right about that."

Dylan reached out and tucked an errant lock of hair behind her ear. She shivered at the contact.

"What happened?" His voice was quiet against the pounding surf.

"His plane went down in some heavy fog. He shouldn't have been flying, the weather report was iffy, but he hadn't been in the air for three days and it was really bugging him. He saw a window of opportunity and headed straight to the airport. But he never made it back."

Silence hung heavy in the air between them, broken only by Carly's soft tones as she chattered a running commentary of her play in the sand a few feet away.

"I'm so sorry." He didn't shift away or show any other signs of discomfort. Just sat with her, quietly, his palm against her shoulder radiating warmth.

She shrugged, not wanting sympathy. "The reports said he didn't feel a thing, that he died instantly. But we were the ones who had to pick up the pieces."

Dylan nodded his understanding. "So the thought of anyone taking a risk, especially when they have a child, pushed some buttons for you."

"Huge buttons," she agreed, smiling ruefully at him.

"I hope you know I'm not like that," he added.

She was silent for a moment. Dylan let out a burst of air, frustration written across his forehead.

"My job may be a little out of the ordinary, but I don't take unnecessary risks. When the conditions aren't right, I stay in. I have a daughter to raise, and I intend to do just that."

"I know. I'm sorry," she said, shoulders relaxing as she finally accepted that he was not a carbon copy of her father. For her dad, the sky had always come first. For Dylan, charter fishing was his job.

"Apology accepted," he said, and this time she knew it really had been.

Satisfied that they had finally made peace with the argument from the night before, Madison relaxed, enjoying the rumble of the surf and the delicate patterns Dylan's fingers were tracing on her shoulder. Even through the thick cardigan her skin tingled.

"So..."

"So," Dylan echoed.

Madison took a deep breath and began to stand. "I should probably go now."

"You don't have to," he said, reaching for her hand.

To her surprise, Madison realized that she wanted to stay. As much as she'd dreaded this conversation, Dylan's calm understanding had gone a long way towards making it as easy as possible.

His fingertips skimmed her knuckles, sending a wave of weakness tumbling through her. She sat back down on the rough log, hoping the movement had disguised the trembling in her knees.

Dylan was looking out at the ocean, his eyes squinting against the play of sunlight on water. The tide, though still far from where they sat, was definitely coming in.

When he spoke, she had to lean in closer to catch his words over the roar of the surf and the rustle of wind. "My dad died my junior year of college."

Madison squeezed his hand; it seemed to be all the encouragement he needed.

"He died on his boat—not in a fishing accident, but from a

heart attack while scrubbing down the decks." He cleared his throat, then continued. "It was pretty touch and go there for a while. Financially, I mean. I took over the charter business during summer break, just to pay the bills and make sure Mom had enough to live on."

"Why not sell the business and live on the profits?"

Dylan snorted. "What profits? This was during the lean years, when he was barely scraping a living. We would have taken a huge hit." He gripped her hand a little tighter. "Besides, he'd built the charter from the ground up, running the business in good times and bad. The boom years helped him put away the money so I could go to college. It didn't feel right to let it go."

"And what about now?"

"What about it?"

"I'm guessing that by majoring in Computer Science, you weren't exactly planning to run the charter business long-term."

Dylan smiled ruefully. "Life doesn't always turn out the way we plan, does it?" He stood, shading his eyes as he stared out at the rolling surf. "Rain's coming in," he observed.

"I didn't mean to..."

He held out his hand, lifted her to her feet. "No big deal. But it's getting late. We'd better head back." He walked the few steps to Carly's side, pulling Madison with him. They both crouched down to get a better look at Carly's sand castle. Holding out his free hand to his daughter, Dylan turned toward home.

Madison quietly let go of Dylan's hand and followed daddy and daughter all the way back to The Inn.

Dinner, dishes, and bedtime were long over by the time Dylan caught a minute to himself. Slipping out of the house to the front porch, he dropped down into the porch swing. The gentle swaying of the swing, coupled with the seasonably warm night air, helped soothe him a bit.

He wasn't sure what exactly had set him off this afternoon in his conversation with Madison. She raised some valid points, hell, more than valid. They were the same things he'd been asking himself ever since his father had died.

As much as he loved the sea, fishing wasn't in his blood. When he left for college, he assumed—as did everyone else—that it would be for good. But when his father died, leaving behind a pile of debt and a charter business desperately needing attention, he hadn't given it a second thought.

But now he was financially secure, and so was his mother. The world of charter fishing was starting to look up again, so he could probably make a tidy profit if he sold *The Lucky Strike*. But something was holding him back.

It had been a real bone of contention between him and Karen, that's for sure. She never understood why he would bury himself in this backwater town, stinking of salt water and fish guts half the year, when he had plenty of opportunity to be a rising star in the bigger cities of the Northwest.

He could still hear her voice, which had grown increasingly shrill during her time in Westport. "Why are you throwing your life away here? You had offers from Microsoft and Google, for God's sake! We could have money. We could live in a real city. We could be *happy*. I don't understand you!"

And that had been the crux of the problem, Dylan mused ruefully. She'd never understood the allure of small town life, never comprehended the responsibility he felt towards his mother, never respected his desire to see his father's dream continue on after his death.

Of course, he'd never really understood Karen and her need for upward mobility, either, so they were even on that point. They'd met and gotten engaged in college, but since she'd married him even after he returned home to Westport, he thought they were on the same page regarding the charter business. But he realized too late that she thought life on the coast was just a blip in his intended climb through the ranks of the computer geniuses.

In a lot of ways, his life here in Westport was the best of all possible worlds. He had close friends and family, a chance to develop his computer business away from the cutthroat environment of the big city where guys with his talent were a dime a dozen. And if he'd gone to work for someone else, his time with Carly would have been slashed dramatically as he put in the hours necessary to be a success.

On the other hand, the charter business took more time away from Carly than he would have liked. And as much as he loved his mother and liked his childhood home, he wished his schedule allowed for him to find a place just for him and his daughter.

Then there was the whole situation with his social life. He hated to admit it, but his life had been pretty solitary since Karen left. He certainly didn't want her back, but some companionship would be nice.

And if that companion happened to have sleek blonde hair, a body to drool over, and a quiet demeanor hiding both a tempting sensuality and an innate shyness, it would be more than nice.

A crunch from the gravel path in front of the porch drew his attention. As if conjured by his thoughts, Madison stood in front of him, dimly lit by the low lighting placed at strategic intervals along the walkway.

"Enjoying an after-dinner walk?" Dylan cleared his throat,

cursing the husky note that had crept in while he was woolgathering. Even to his own ears, it sounded like an invitation to something illicit. And much as he was attracted to her, that wasn't what he wanted from a short-timer like Madison.

Was it?

"Partly," she replied. "Plus, I wanted to return your coat." As she handed it over the railing to him, the crinkle of paper caught his ear. She held a well-read copy of the local newsweekly in her other hand.

Noting the path of his look, Madison glanced down, almost seeming surprised to find the paper there. "I, uh, was reading the *Westport Weekly*," she continued.

"Mm-hmm." Dylan waited for her to continue, folding the jacket over his arm.

She looked at the paper, the treetops, the edge of the path as it curved around the bend. Several times she opened her mouth as if to speak, but stopped herself. Finally, she looked him straight in the eye and blurted out, "Are you busy Thursday night?"

"I–uh–" Was Madison actually asking him out on a date? "I don't think so. Why?"

Madison held the newspaper out in front of her like a shield. "There's an article about a silent auction for the Chamber of Commerce. I'd like to go, but I think I'd feel a little awkward on my own."

Well. It wasn't the most passionate of requests, but Dylan was pleased nonetheless. Despite his reservations, he was growing more and more attracted to Madison every day. A chance to spend an evening with her—even one surrounded by half the town—was an opportunity he didn't want to miss.

"Sounds great. The silent auction is always lots of fun. How about I pick you up at seven?"

Madison nodded, smiled a quirky, shy smile, and turned to

go. A few steps down the path, she stopped to toss a "thanks" over her shoulder.

Dylan sat in the dark and watched her walk away. She was a puzzle, this quiet woman wrapped in the trappings of the big city. But thanks to her rapidly-approaching departure date, he was fairly certain he wouldn't get the chance to unwrap her.

Either way he interpreted that statement, he regretted the lost opportunity.

Chapter Ten

L ight blazed from every window of the community center, and the rumble of conversation could be heard even from the parking lot. As they walked up the steps to the wide front porch, Madison placed a hand on Dylan's arm.

"Are you sure I'm dressed okay?" She waved her free hand at her outfit, a look of panic flashing across her features. "I didn't know what to wear, and I'm afraid..."

Dylan reached over and pressed a finger to her lips. God, they were so soft! If he didn't watch himself, he'd drag her around back and press her up against the wall of the building, diving for her mouth with all the pent-up desire that had been building since she first sashayed down the docks on her way to the charter trip.

"You look beautiful," he said, his voice low and husky with banked need. He took his hand away from her mouth, unwilling to keep playing with fire with so many potential witnesses. Instead, he contented himself with tucking an errant strand of glossy blonde hair behind her ear before shoving his hands into his pockets to resist temptation.

And she was definitely tempting. Her dress was modest; some might even call it conservative, but for the way it poured over her slim form like liquid. The raspberry silk clung from neckline to waist, flaring out over her hips to drape artfully at mid-calf. When she moved, the fabric twirled around her legs, catching the light and drawing the eye.

Dylan scowled a little at the thought of all the eyes that would be following Madison tonight.

"You're frowning," she observed, touching the tip of a neatly manicured finger to the space between his brows. A spark of heat traveled between them.

Dylan quickly smoothed out his facial expression. "Just thinking. No, you've got nothing to worry about outfit-wise. You look perfect." Flashing her a wide smile, he linked his hand with hers and tugged her through the door into the building.

The auditorium-sized room was filled with people, dressed in everything from formalwear to jeans and flannel shirts. Small groups gathered in clumps around the perimeter of the room, drinking punch out of paper cups and chatting.

Several rows of cafeteria-style tables graced the center of the room. The items up for bid in the silent auction were displayed here, and attendees wandered through the rows inspecting the offerings, occasionally jotting down a bid on the sheets of paper in front of each item.

"Drink?" Dylan had to raise his voice to be heard over the din. At Madison's nod, he guided her to the refreshments table, situated at the far side of the room.

It was the same every year, he mused as he ladled punch into a pair of cups. The decorations were heavy on the crepe paper and balloons, in shades of blue and green to reflect the nautical theme. The refreshments table held the mayor's huge glass punch bowl and two dishes of party mints; after dinner, an array of desserts would join them.

The room had more of a homecoming dance atmosphere than a fancy fundraising event, but it raised a surprising amount of money every year. And it suited the town.

Handing Madison her cup, he took a sip from his own and looked around. Yes, everything in the room suited Westport, from the eclectic mix of attendees to the range of items up for bid. Where else could you bid on a romantic dinner at the only fancy restaurant in town and a hull-scraping for your boat at the same time?

"Dylan!"

Dylan groaned inwardly as the heavyset, middle-aged woman beamed at him, waving enthusiastically as she made her way through the crowds. His hand slid into Madison's almost unconsciously, twining his fingers with hers.

"Oh, Dylan, don't you look handsome!" She reached up and pinched his cheek, her features scrunched into a kissy-face look. "I was telling your mother just the other day that you're looking more handsome all the time. And your daughter is just precious." She glanced over her shoulder, searching the room. "Alexis is in town, you know. She was just promoted to head of the European division, the youngest in the history of the company..."

Dylan interrupted before she could go any further. "Mrs. Williams, may I introduce Madison McIntyre? Madison, this is Cassie Williams, one of my mother's closest friends and chairperson for the silent auction." *And partner in crime when it came to matchmaking*, he added silently.

"Nice to meet you, my dear," Mrs. Williams said, holding out her hand to Madison. The cheerful expression on her face fell just a little bit as she noticed that Madison had to let go of Dylan's hand to shake with her. It disappeared completely when Madison linked her fingers with Dylan's again after the greeting.

"My pleasure," Madison said, smiling politely. "The auction seems wonderful so far. You've done a great job."

Dylan glanced sideways at Madison, but her expression was open and sincere. Although she had to be used to the more formal events a city like Seattle had to offer, she seemed to be honestly enjoying herself.

Cassie Williams thawed a little at Madison's praise. "I'm glad you're having a good time. Dylan, don't forget to look up Alexis while you're here," she said, and forged her way through the crowds again.

Madison glanced up at Dylan, thick lashes shadowing her eyes. "Alexis?" Her raspberry-slicked lips curved into a teasing smile.

Dylan grimaced. "Our moms have been trying to get us together since we were kids. Something about wanting to be in-laws as well as best friends."

"Dylan!"

Speak of the devil, he thought as he turned around. Alexis was crossing the room to where he and Madison stood. She was dressed, as usual, impeccably, looking like someone who just stepped off a fashion runway in Milan.

She stopped just in front of him and held out her hands. Grasping his hands, she leaned forward and kissed him, Continental-style, on both cheeks. "Hello, darling! So glad to see you!"

"Nice you could make it to your mom's big party," Dylan answered, subtly extricating his hands from hers and placing one arm not-so-subtly around Madison's waist. "Alexis, I'd like you to meet Madison McIntyre."

Alexis barreled right over his introduction, gracing

Madison with a brief glance. "It wasn't easy, with my schedule. I just flew in from Paris."

Dylan heard Madison mutter something that sounded like "and boy are my arms tired," and he clenched his jaw to hold back the laughter that threatened.

"But I promised Mom I'd be here for the auction, so here I am. And counting the minutes until I'm out of Westport again." Alexis glanced over her shoulder at the gathered crowd. "Darling, how can you stand it here? You should be living somewhere exciting."

"Westport is about as exciting as I want," he said nonchalantly. Out of the corner of his eye, he saw Madison give a little head-bob in agreement.

"I'd choose Westport over a big city any day," Madison added, smiling at Alexis' disbelieving expression. "It's much more relaxed, and the people are wonderful."

Alexis looked pointedly at Madison's waist, where Dylan's hand rested comfortably. "I suppose there are incentives."

"Yes, there are." Dylan wrapped his arm more firmly around Madison. "It's been nice seeing you again, Alexis," he said, "But I promised Madison we'd take a look at the auction items before bidding closed. Maybe we'll run into each other later."

"That was slick," Madison said once they were out of earshot, a teasing note in her voice.

"She's a nice person, but you can see why Mom's matchmaking never took. She's definitely not my type."

Madison pushed a stray lock of hair behind her ear. "And just what is your type?"

Dylan's steps slowed. This was a new side of Madison, a teasing, almost flirtatious side. And if he'd been attracted to the shy, studious Madison before, he was completely lost now. "I think I'll take the Fifth," he finally said.

Madison glanced at him sideways. "Smart man," she murmured.

"Hungry?"

Madison looked up at Dylan and smiled. "Starving," she admitted. They had been at the auction for over an hour now, and her stomach was starting to voice its discomfort rather loudly.

"Then let's go take our seats. Dinner should be served any minute now."

Dylan introduced her to the others sitting with them; it seemed as though he knew everyone. One of the benefits of living in a small town, Madison thought.

She'd been to fundraisers before, mostly out of business obligations, and had always felt awkward and out of place. Even surrounded by her co-workers, she had never felt comfortable at the events she attended as required by Donovan Developers.

But this was something different altogether. The few people she'd met in Westport had gone out of their way to say hello and see if she was having a good time. And the amazing thing was, she was pretty sure they meant it.

And, of course, spending time with Dylan was no hardship either. She snuck a look at him, her breath catching in her throat. In tailored slacks or well-worn jeans, the man never failed to look amazing.

But his looks were just the icing on the cake. It was his personality, the way his mind worked, the devotion he had towards his daughter—all one tempting package that she wished she could keep.

Maybe forever.

Oh, my goodness. Was she falling in love with him?

A high school student dressed in waitstaff black and white slid a full plate onto the table in front of her, diverting her from the disturbing trend of her thoughts. Madison dug in to the food, grateful for the distraction.

"This is amazing!" Madison took a sip of punch, staring with disbelief at the plate in front of her. "I've never tasted salmon this good before!"

"Fresh caught," Dylan pointed out, with not a little pride. "The only way to eat seafood."

"I can see why," she agreed, forking up another bite. She closed her eyes as she savored the taste.

"The rice pilaf isn't bad, either," Dylan said, offering her a taste.

Her lips closed around the spoon, her mouth suddenly dry as her eyes locked with his. She swallowed automatically, barely tasting the rice. "Delicious," she murmured.

Time slowed; she watched his Adam's apple bob up and down as he swallowed. And was that a tiny scar at the edge of his mouth?

Suddenly aware of the people surrounding them, Madison broke eye contact first. Ears burning, she turned her attention back to the food.

Dinner was followed by fresh berry cobbler and coffee, and Madison spent an enjoyable half hour meeting and chatting with the other people at their table. From time to time, she caught Dylan looking at her with an expression that made her insides cartwheel. She was pretty sure her heart rate didn't go down the entire meal.

Once the dishes had been cleared, the emcee for the evening took over at the podium. One by one, people came forward to pick up their gift certificates or the actual items, carrying them back to their tables with wide grins on their faces.

"The next item offered is a romantic dinner for two at the Lighthouse Restaurant." The emcee flourished the gift certificate in front of him. "The lucky winner is sure to score some points for this one! And the top bid goes to ... Dylan Edwards!"

The woman next to Madison nudged her as Dylan retrieved his certificate. "Way to go, honey!" she said. "There's not a single woman in this room who wouldn't give her eyeteeth for a date at the Lighthouse with Dylan. And even a couple of married ones!"

Madison blushed. "Oh, I don't think he got it with me in mind," she demurred.

Her seatmate let out a bark of laughter. "Right," she drawled. A wide grin spread over her face as Dylan joined them again. "Nice bid," she said, leaning across Madison to nudge Dylan good-naturedly.

Thoroughly embarrassed, Madison glanced sideways at Dylan. He looked quite satisfied with himself, tucking the gift certificate in the inside pocket of his sports jacket.

He caught her looking and raised one eyebrow. "It's a great restaurant. You should try it sometime."

Thankfully, Madison was saved from a reply by the emcee, who had moved on to the next item. "And now the final item of the evening! The lucky winner will enjoy a weekend at The Inn, Westport's premier bed and breakfast establishment. And the winner is..." He paused for a moment, brow furrowing as he double-checked the paperwork. "Ladies and gentlemen, I apologize for the delay. There's a bit of an unusual situation here. The top bidder evidently wants his or her identity concealed. Well, I'm not one to argue with the top bid of the entire evening!"

A round of applause met his announcement. He continued,

"We will be sending the gift certificate to the lucky bidder tomorrow. And I suppose we'll all find out who it is when they cash in the prize, right?"

Laughter greeted this last comment, and the emcee added a few final words before relinquishing the podium.

"Well, that was odd," Dylan said, casually placing an arm around the back of Madison's chair.

"Hmm," Madison replied, attention more focused on the heat circling her shoulders than the conversational topic.

"I don't think a bidder has ever remained anonymous at one of these auctions," he continued.

Madison shrugged. "At least it gave everyone something to talk about besides your bid," she said.

Dylan laughed softly. "Now I want to find out who the mystery person is even more."

"Why is that?"

"I'd like to thank him in person."

One luxury Dylan's car lacked was an adequate heater. Madison pulled her wrap tighter, shivering a little.

Dylan shook his head. "Sorry. How about we take a dip in the hot tub to warm up after we get back?"

"Oh, I don't know..."

He stretched his arm over the back of the car seat. "You don't have the bathing suit excuse anymore."

She was sure that even in the dim interior of the car he could see her blushing. A charged silence filled the car.

"This isn't the way back to The Inn." Madison squinted out the window. "Are you taking a short cut?"

"More like a long cut." Dylan flicked a look at Madison, then turned his attention back to the unpaved road. "I've had a great time tonight and I'm not in the mood to say good night yet. So if you're not interested in the hot tub, how about Wash-away Beach?"

Madison looked down at her outfit. "I'm not really dressed for walking on the beach," she said.

"Actually, I was talking more about looking than walking." He pulled the car into an empty lot at the top of a cliff and killed the engine. "This is the scenic viewpoint right above the beach."

"Dylan Edwards," she said with a mock frown. "Are you telling me you've brought me to a makeout spot?"

Moonlight shone down on the water below, sparking indigo and crystal as the waves tumbled and crashed. The low rumble of the surf was barely audible in the car's interior.

"Hell, yes." He turned toward her, a bad boy grin on his face. "I've been wanting to do this all night."

Dylan slid across the bench seat, tucking his arm more firmly around Madison. She sighed, snuggling into the curve of his arm. With a muttered oath Dylan shifted, lifting her chin with one hand before claiming her mouth with his own.

His tongue traced the seam of her lips, and she opened eagerly to him. He tasted of berries and chocolate, more intoxicating than champagne. She placed a hand on his chest, just below his collarbone; heat radiated through his dress shirt.

He captured her head with one broad hand; the other traced the neckline of her dress, eliciting a shudder of desire from her that echoed in the pulse she could feel under her palm.

Her fingers raked through his hair as their tongues danced and sparred. He moved his hand lower, palming her breast, and Madison responded with a soft moan. Her breathing escalated with each delicate touch. Who would have thought a strong man like Dylan could have such gentle hands? She arched into his touch, urging him on.

That was all the encouragement he needed. With a swift motion, he tugged down her zipper and slid the dress from her shoulders. And through it all they continued to kiss, long, heated, drugging kisses that made her head whirl and body pulse in frustrated longing. Dylan slid one hand around to cup her breast, the warmth of his strong, calloused fingers branding her. He stroked her through the lace of her bra, beading her nipple and pulling a strangled cry from her. She wanted...she needed...

Then he pulled back, breathing heavily, his forehead resting against hers as he fought to regain control.

"I feel like a teenager at the submarine races," he said, tipping his head towards the fogged windshield.

Madison stared at him, sure her brain had disconnected during the past few minutes. "Submarine races?" she echoed.

Dylan laughed softly, stroking her hair away from her face. "That's what we used to call it when we went parking. Watching the submarine races."

Madison nodded, a smile tugging at her lips. "So who's winning?"

He traced one finger along her collarbone, teasing at the edge of lace on her demi-bra. "I think I am."

Emboldened, she slid off first one bra strap, then the other. A flick of the wrist at the front clasp opened it fully.

The heat in his eyes flared even brighter as moonlight played over her rosy-tipped breasts. "Damn," he breathed, before circling one taut nipple with his forefinger.

She quivered under his touch, then cried out as he dipped his head and took her nipple into his mouth.

Heat surrounded her, sending a pulsing need straight to her core. She threaded her fingers through his dark hair, holding him close. He switched his attentions to her other breast, his hands stroking down her back.

Suddenly, he lifted his head. His eyes were dark. "You're wearing too many clothes," he growled.

"So are you," she said in a breathless voice she barely recognized as her own. Scrabbling at his shirt, she pulled it free and stripped it off over his head. Then she took a moment to look at him.

Yep. There was that chest she'd been dreaming about since their night in the hot tub.

Sighing with pleasure, she spread her hands wide on his heated chest, reveling in the feeling of taut muscle under hair-dusted skin. He shuddered as her fingers trailed down to the waistband of his pants.

Gripping her wrists in his strong hands, he held her slightly away. "Any more exploring and I'll be done before we get started." Reaching over the back of the seat, he grabbed a blanket and folded it. Then he placed it against the passenger door, made sure the door was locked, and reached for Madison again.

He gently positioned her so she leaned against the blanket, her body turned sideways on the seat. "God, I love bench seats," he said, before leaning over her to take her mouth in another drugging kiss.

Her lips were swollen and parted when he finally broke away, both of them breathing hard. He kissed her once more, then moved down her body, slowly drawing off her dress as he went.

She shivered as he pulled the soft fabric off, leaving her naked but for the skimpy panties she'd splurged on during her quick trip back to Seattle.

Thank heavens she had. Utilitarian cotton undies wouldn't have quite the same effect, judging by the flare of heat in his eyes.

Then again, she amended as he hooked his fingers in the sides of the French bikini-cut silk panties and removed them, too, maybe it didn't really matter what she wore.

A part of her was embarrassed to be sprawled naked on the front seat of his sedan. But even that small flare of nerves disappeared in a wave of pleasure that rolled over her as he lifted her legs over his shoulders and leaned forward to taste her.

Oh, God. She writhed under his ministrations, her head whipping from side to side as he explored her with his fingers, his mouth, his tongue. He slid one finger inside her as his tongue swirled around her clit, drawing a sobbing cry from her throat. She grabbed the arm rest with one hand, the back of the seat with the other, as he drove her closer and closer to that elusive peak.

Panting, groaning, she gave herself over to the waves of heat spiraling through her body. "Come for me," he whispered, his voice harsh with need. He thrust two fingers inside as he sucked her clit into his mouth.

She arched her back as the orgasm crashed through her, sobbing his name as tremors shook her from head to toe. His touch gentled as he brought her back down from the cresting wave, little pulsing aftershocks traveling through her.

Finally, finally they slowed enough so she could catch her breath, gasping pants that echoed in the close confines of the car. He straightened, taking her by the hand to tug her into his arms. She leaned against him, her body limp, as she willed her heart to stop pounding.

"I can't believe..." She couldn't complete the thought, wasn't sure if she'd ever be able to have a coherent thought again.

"I know."

And the funny thing was, she believed him. He did know her. In all the ways it counted.

She turned in his arms and pressed a kiss to the underside of his jaw.

"We can't stay here." There was a note of regret in his voice as they started out the foggy window at the crashing surf below.

"I know." With trembling fingers, she retrieved her dress and underwear. It wouldn't do to get caught in the front seat of Dylan's car without her clothes on.

But she wasn't ready for tonight to be over. Not by a long shot.

Dylan watched her, a small frown creasing his forehead. "Is everything okay?"

She nodded shakily, her eyes trained steadily on his face. "Let's go back to my cabin," she whispered.

Back at The Inn, Dylan pulled into the tiny parking area behind the cabins and parked. Her clothing may have been put back in some semblance of order, but Madison's hair was disheveled beyond repair. Hopefully they would make it to her cabin without being seen.

Dylan was still half-amazed that Madison had invited him back to her place, but judging by the speed with which she unbuckled her seat belt it appeared that she hadn't changed her mind on the short drive. He followed her lead and got out of the car.

Once on the path, he grabbed her hand and started towards the cabin, the two of them practically running in their haste to get inside. Madison stumbled on a rock, slowing down temporarily, but just giggled and flashed a wide smile at Dylan. His heart stuttered as he glimpsed her beauty once again.

Tonight at the auction he'd finally accepted that Madison was nothing like his ex-wife. Her city-slicker label had been a handy excuse, but untrue. Madison had fit in like she'd been a small-town resident all her life.

It was especially noticeable when he compared her to Alexis. His childhood acquaintance, born and bred in Westport, had skipped town right after graduation and was now as big city as they came.

So maybe it all came down to personality. And Madison's personality, he admitted, was one he wanted to have in his life.

Maybe even on a permanent basis.

At the bottom of the steps, Dylan reached for Madison's hands, pulling her close for another kiss. As his lips descended to hers, a voice broke the silence.

"It's about time you got back, Madison."

Chapter Eleven

"Madison?" Dylan looked from Madison to the man standing on her porch and back again. Her face had drained of all color, a stricken expression marring her delicate features. She was staring at the stranger, horror in her eyes.

"B-bob?" She mumbled, her gaze never leaving the man on the porch. Okay, obviously not a stranger to her. "What are you doing here?"

"Waiting for you, of course," Bob snapped, ostentatiously checking his watch. Dylan wouldn't place money on it, but the thick gold band screamed "Rolex" to him. "Do you have any idea how long I've been standing on this godforsaken porch?"

"You needn't have bothered." Madison flicked a glance at Dylan. The tension was thicker than the pea-soup fog that had drifted ashore.

"Well, if I'd known you'd be out carousing with the locals, I would have shown up a lot sooner," Bob snarled.

Madison shrank back. "We weren't carousing. I was..."

Dylan stopped her with a hand on her shoulder. "I'm sorry,

but we haven't been introduced. And I'm not sure exactly what sort of relationship you two have where Madison feels the need to explain an evening out."

Bob gave a short bark of laughter, derision on his face. "Relationship? With the ice princess? Not hardly. You couldn't pay me enough. I'm Bob Lee, Madison's boss."

Dylan took the proffered hand, barely hiding his distaste at the other man's limp-fish handshake. "Dylan Edwards. You must have pretty urgent business to discuss if you had to come all the way out to the coast during Madison's sabbatical."

"Sabbatical?" Bob snorted. "Is that what she told you?"

"Bob," Madison warned, taking a step forward.

"Although if this is an example of what she's been doing here, it doesn't surprise me," he continued, giving her a nasty look.

Dylan glanced from one to the other, a sensation of unease growing in his stomach. "Would someone tell me what the hell is going on?"

"Please, Dylan, I'll explain later," Madison said, steering him towards the path to home.

"Tell him now," Bob said. "Hell, everyone's going to know sooner or later." When Madison didn't answer, he said, "She's putting together the new resort plan for Donovan Development."

"How dare you," Madison hissed as she grabbed Bob by the sleeve and hauled him into the cabin, slamming the door behind them. Dylan was already gone, with a mumbled excuse about looking in on his daughter. But the look on his face had left an ache in Madison's heart.

"Watch it. Armani," Bob warned, plucking her fingers off

his coat sleeve and brushing at the wrinkled fabric. "How dare I what? Check on your progress? Interrupt your little love nest? Tell the truth?"

Madison stalked across the room and hefted her files onto the table. "I brought you a progress report a week ago and have been checking in regularly by phone and e-mail. As you can tell by the amount of research I have here on the table, I've been working almost around the clock, so this would hardly qualify as a love nest. And by telling the truth you've probably ruined my chances of success on this project– although I'd bet that was your intention in the first place." She knew she was treading on dangerous ground, but she didn't care. The anger was roaring out of every pore, and it felt—good. Liberating. Cleansing. After so much time spent holding in her rage towards Bob, it was inevitable she would reach a boiling point. She just never expected it to be here.

"Oh, please." Bob inspected the seat at the table before sitting, his nose wrinkling with distaste. "As if I don't have better things to do than plot your demise. You really need to get over yourself. And if you thought a lame excuse like a sabbatical would cover you while you worked on the resort plans, you're more out of touch than I thought."

In response, Madison walked over to the door and opened it. "Good night, Bob."

"Touchy, touchy."

"We can continue this discussion tomorrow." She swept an arm towards the open door.

"Over breakfast," he tossed over his shoulder as he walked outside. "I'm staying in the cabin next door."

Madison glared at his back until he was safely off the porch. Then she slammed the door and stood in the entryway, shaking with pent-up adrenaline.

Her little outburst had probably cost her any chance at a

promotion in Donovan—but, to be honest, she had little chance of that anyway. Even if the resort went through, she still was too much on the outside to move up.

Of course, when the company chose people like Bob for the fast track, she had to wonder whether she really wanted to be part of that inner circle anyway.

More than her job prospects, though, Madison was sick about the lost opportunity with Dylan. She'd been so close to opening her heart, sharing something intensely intimate with him. Now that chance was lost forever.

How could he forgive her for lying about something so important? It wasn't like she hadn't had opportunities to bring it up–oh, say, when he'd talked about Westport development, or when they were at Washaway. At least before deciding to make love with him.

Madison threw herself down on the bed, gripping a pillow over her head. Her gaze fell, unbidden, on the half-opened package next to her bed. Maybe she should go for a dip in the hot tub, after all...

No. Not now. Especially not before she had a chance to see Dylan, apologize for withholding the truth. Even the off-chance that she'd run in to him there was enough to put that option on hold.

But if she ever set things right with him, all bets were off.

"Regular or decaf?" Ronnie Edwards was missing her trademark smile as she waited for Madison's reply. With a nod, she filled the mug and retreated to the kitchen.

"Friendly people, huh?" Bob wiped his mouth with a napkin and helped himself to another cruller. "At least the food is tolerable."

Madison shot him her best evil-death-ray glare and continued picking at her cinnamon swirl French toast. It was delicious, as usual, but she couldn't seem to work up much of an appetite this morning.

"Later today we need to sit down and go over your proposal in-depth. I assume you've scheduled your presentation?"

"I'm on the agenda for the next city council meeting, one week from today."

"Wonderful. I'll see you there."

Madison's head flew up at the sound of Dylan's voice.

He was leaning against one of the hardwood pillars that framed the entrance to the dining room, his arms crossed. A long-sleeved tee-shirt clung to every muscle, outlining the power in his arms and chest. Second-skin jeans molded his hips and thighs, a small rip at the knee just hinting at the possibilities.

Madison swallowed. "You go to the city council meetings?" Mentally, she slapped her forehead. Could she sound any more inane?

Dylan shrugged. "They usually prefer that city council members show up once in a while."

Oh, no. Madison closed her eyes briefly.

"But then, I'm sure you knew that," Dylan continued, his gaze never leaving her face. "All part of your plan."

"I don't have a plan," Madison protested.

Bob snorted. "Just what every boss wants to hear from a subordinate."

"No! I mean, I do have a plan, but not the way you meant, Dylan. I never meant to mislead you—"

"So that business about the sabbatical was totally on the up and up, right?"

"No, but—"

"I've gotta go." Dylan slapped on a baseball cap and pushed away from the pillar. "You can save your excuses for later."

And with that, he was gone.

"Hey, man, watch yourself." John stepped back, a wrinkle of disgust on his face. "You're getting fish guts all over me."

"Sorry." Dylan shifted slightly so his cleaning efforts would run directly off the boat, instead of over his assistant's feet. He scooped up another bucket of water and slopped it along the deck.

John stomped off, muttering to himself about moronic bosses who couldn't get their heads on straight.

Dylan sighed and sloshed more water on the deck, washing off the detritus of the day. Then he grabbed a push broom and started scrubbing.

At least while the boat was underway he didn't have time to think. Too busy riding the waves, watching the weather, assisting customers in their quest for the big one. But now that they were back in port, the mindless repetition of the clean-up routine left him plenty of time to stew.

It was unfortunate that the weather had forced a postponement of the charter trip this morning. Walking into the dining room and seeing Madison and her smarmy, snarky boss sitting there together nearly blew his carefully-maintained composure.

He shook his head and attacked a particularly nasty stretch of decking. By the time he was done, *The Lucky Strike* would be the shiniest boat in the harbor.

Bilious Bob had set his teeth on edge from the moment he first saw him. Fancy clothes, superior attitude, and a nasty streak barely hidden by his sheen of polite society. He'd been offended on Madison's behalf —until her dirty little secret came out.

Dylan stopped, resting on the broom handle for a moment. He should have known. In a way, he *did* know, with her secretive manner and constant "research". And he'd always known she wasn't the sort to fit in here for any extended period of time.

But the knowledge that she'd been using him, using his family, in order to advance her career, really smarted. She was practically Karen's twin in that regard.

Of course, she had to have known about his city council position. How long had she been milking him for information, spending time with him to plan out her strategy?

He'd been such a fool.

He couldn't trust her. And even worse, he couldn't trust his own judgment.

Swearing under his breath, he attacked the deck with renewed vigor. Another bucket of water washed away the last of the grime.

"Hey!" John's head popped up from below decks. "I just finished down here! Watch where you're slopping that stuff!"

Dylan shoved the baseball cap back and scratched his head. "Go ahead and take off, man. I'll finish up."

"Don't have to ask me twice." The gangly young man swung himself up the narrow stairs and crossed the deck, managing the slippery planks easily. "See ya tomorrow."

With a wave, Dylan sent him off. A quick inspection showed that everything was in order for the next morning. Popping below decks for a moment, he grabbed some paperwork and locked up the cabin.

He exited the boat and checked the lines one last time, pleased to see the professional job John had done before leaving for the day. In the three years John had been crewing for him, he'd turned into a fine seaman.

A low whistle from a nearby boat caught his attention and he looked up. From his vantage point crouched down next to the anchoring lines, he had a perfect view of a perfect set of legs, clad in trim khaki Capri's. His gaze skimmed higher, catching briefly on the curve of her hips, the rich blue blouse tucked into her waistband, the modest neckline only hinting at the curves beneath.

Even now, as angry as he was, his body responded to her presence. He gritted his teeth and silently cursed his libido. How could he want her after what she had done?

"Hello." She stood quietly, the only indication of her nervousness the twisting and untwisting of the strap on her purse.

He nodded, rising slowly to match and then exceed her height. At this point, he was angry enough to use the advantages at his disposal. Height was one. Silence was another.

The pause worked. Madison glanced away, swallowing visibly at the pitch and roll of the boat anchored for the night. Then she looked back, squaring her shoulders and meeting his eye for the first time since she arrived.

"I think we need to talk."

Dylan shrugged. "Not much to talk about."

"I need to talk."

Another shrug. "Suit yourself."

Madison let out a frustrated little puff of air. "May I buy you a cup of coffee?"

He started down the dock towards shore, leaving her to trail behind him, picking her way along the swaying dock. "Fine. But let's make it quick. I need to get home to my daughter."

"Of course."

Silence reigned as they reached shore and headed down the main street of town. At the Seafood Shack, she lifted an eyebrow at him, which he answered with a nod.

Apart from a few waves, most of the patrons ignored their entrance, leaving them some privacy as they headed for the table in the back. Dylan slid into the booth and tossed his cap on the seat next to him. Susie noted their arrival and started to round the counter, but he stopped her with a raised hand and a request for two coffees.

"You wanted to talk," he prompted. No need to drag this whole messy thing out longer than necessary.

"I wanted to explain the situation," she replied. Her purse strap had been replaced by a napkin in her nervous twisting. "I never meant to mislead you."

"Interesting choice of words." Dylan accepted the steaming mug of coffee with murmured thanks, sipping at the scalding brew.

Madison added cream and sugar to hers before taking an exploratory sip. "I honestly had no idea you were on the city council. I never even considered the possibility."

"Too ignorant? Too blue-collar?"

"Too young," she shot back. "Most council members I've met in the past have been closer to retirement age."

"Well, that's a sweeping generalization," he said.

"Obviously," she muttered. "And an incorrect one, as it turns out. But it's the truth."

"The truth. Another interesting subject. Why did you lie about the reason you were here?"

She looked away. "I was afraid I'd lose my job."

"You'd get fired for telling the truth?"

"I'll get fired if I don't get this resort deal to go through."

"Then take some advice, Madison. Start updating your resume. Because Westport will never approve a resort plan by Donovan Developers."

This time, everyone turned to watch as Dylan stormed out of the café.

Chapter Twelve

Well, that had gone swimmingly. Madison pulled a few bills out of her purse and dropped them on the table, more than enough to cover the cost of the coffee and a generous tip. At least when the rest of the town learned the truth, she'd have one mark in her favor—a record of extravagant tipping.

Weighed against her faults, it didn't seem particularly favorable.

Her time in Westport had taken off her blinders just a little bit, and she wasn't sure she liked what she saw in the mirror. Someone overly focused on work, to the exclusion of any sort of social life. A person afraid to take risks, more interested in standing in place than breaking out of her shell.

For so many years she had taken the cautious route, warned away from risks by her father's example. But in so doing, she now realized to her chagrin that she had turned into her mother—nervous, withdrawn, on the road to bitter.

She checked her watch and hurried out the door, dreading the meeting with Bob that was scheduled in five minutes. He'd commandeered all her research for the day, insisting he needed to read through everything in order to "get a feel for it." Now they were going to discuss it at length.

Madison felt like a kid on the verge of the most important pop quiz of her life.

Back at The Inn, she detoured around her cabin and headed for the one next door. Knowing that Bob was staying so close made her skin crawl. She'd suggested the library, but he'd whined about professional privacy, as if spies would be lurking in the new book section.

Bob answered at the first knock, motioning her in as he returned to the table, which was strewn with her paperwork. "Have a seat," he muttered.

She looked around, stumped at the prospect of finding a clear surface to sit on. The room looked like a paper recycling plant had exploded—files, maps, brochures, and computer print-outs covered every possible inch of the table, chairs, bed, and nightstand. Bob even had stacks of paper lined up on the kitchen counter. Madison wouldn't have been surprised to find a topographical map in the sink.

Finally she transferred some papers from a kitchen chair to the floor and sat, waiting for Bob to finish whatever it was he was working on.

He ignored her for several minutes, checking figures from one page and making changes on another. Finally, he set them aside and sat back, steepling his fingers under his chin.

Madison shifted uncomfortably under his gaze. *Might as well bite the bullet*, she thought. "What did you think?"

Bob shrugged. "Decent research effort. Could use some organizational help."

Madison glanced at the wreckage of her research strewn around his room and swallowed back a biting remark.

"But you obviously have no idea what makes a Donovan Development resort. I'm just glad I got here in time."

"In time for what?"

"You are no longer responsible for the Westport project. I have orders from the Board of Directors to take over and complete the work you started. You can go back to Seattle now —tonight, if you like."

Madison's face whitened. "You can't do this."

Bob started packing away the research she had worked so hard to compile. "It's already done."

"But—but my job..."

"You still have a job, at least for the time being. And if this project flies, I'll be sure to put in a good word for you."

Her fingers curled into fists. "You arrogant, sneaky, low-down..."

Bob held up a warning hand. "You're on thin ice as it is, Madison. Watch yourself."

"I'll go to the board."

"Like they'll listen to you," he sneered. "Now get out. You're no longer on the company expense account. And you'd better not be late for work tomorrow."

"I—I can't just go now. I can't leave without giving notice. Ronnie is depending on the rent for the rest of the month."

"She's a big girl. It's not like no one's ever skipped out early on a reservation here. I can't even imagine why anyone would stay more than a night in this horrible backwoods place, anyway."

"You're not staying either?"

"Not here." He shuddered. "There's a decent hotel back inland about thirty miles. I have reservations there. So I guess they're losing two customers tonight."

Madison's head was whirling, bombarded with so many

horrible announcements. He might say her job was safe for now, but she knew better. If she showed up at Donovan's tomorrow, the only thing she'd get would be a free box to pack up her office.

And Bob wasn't concerned about the quality of her proposal. He had always wanted this to be a failure for her. If there were a chance it wouldn't fly, he would have been patting her on the back and encouraging her on the path down the gangplank. No, it had to be a solid plan. He was afraid she was going to succeed.

And what better way to avoid that than to swoop in, pronounce her work flawed, and take all the credit for himself.

Bob was still dumping paperwork into cardboard boxes, cheerfully ignoring her. The jerk was actually whistling as he stole her work.

Madison whirled on him, shaking with anger. "Fine. Take my research, take the last three weeks of my life, take my expense account. You can even take my job for all I care. But I'll bet you anything that you won't succeed. And I'm looking forward to watching you fail."

"So I guess I can consider that your two week's notice, give or take a couple of weeks?"

Madison gave him a tight smile. "Consider it my official resignation, effective immediately."

And with a final toss of her hair, she slammed out the door.

Dylan was in the family room playing tea party with Carly when Madison's boss blew in the front door and began pounding on the bell attached to the front desk. Grimacing, Dylan told Carly to stay put and walked into the foyer.

"Does everything move slowly in this town? Some of us

have schedules to keep, you know," Bob grumbled, drumming his fingers on the desktop.

Dylan stopped behind the desk and rested his hands, palm down, on the registration book. "What can I do for you?"

"Just close out my account. I'm leaving tonight, and I want to make sure you don't slip extra charges on my bill." Bob straightened his suit jacket, eyes darting around the room.

"I'm sure you will find everything in order," Dylan said, his teeth aching from biting back the comments he wanted to make.

Bob scrutinized the paperwork, then signed it carelessly and tossed it back on the desk. Reaching down for his suitcase, he turned to go. Stopping suddenly, he looked over his shoulder at Dylan. "Oh, and close out Madison's account, too. She's no longer with Donovan Development, and we won't pay for any more expenses."

Dylan felt the impact like a body blow. Something was definitely wrong here. "What do you mean, she's no longer with Donovan?"

"Good riddance to bad rubbish, I say." Bob shrugged. "She wasn't pulling her weight."

She hadn't been exaggerating the risks, Dylan realized. She really had lost her job over this project. And instead of listening when she tried to apologize, he'd been angry and judgmental. "Where is she now?"

Bob gave him an incredulous look. "You really think I care? You're the one messing around with her, although I'll never understand why. You find her." And with a final sniff, he was out the door.

Dylan ran a hand through his hair, trying to make sense of this turn of events. If Bob was any indicator of the work environment she'd had to endure, no wonder she had gone to such lengths to conceal her reason for being in Westport. Her fear of losing her job had turned out to be very real—and he had tossed it back in her face, along with her apology.

His anger at her lies faded as he realized she would be leaving Westport at any moment. Her job was gone, and so was her reason for being here in the first place. And he'd made it clear to her that he was unwilling to forgive and forget.

Passing through the family room, he smoothed Carly's curls and told her to stay put while he got Grandma. He needed to find Madison–and soon.

Madison heard Dylan's approach well before she saw him. His even, confident strides echoed through the wooded area near the clearing where she sat, back against a rough-barked pine. His footsteps altered from a crunch to a thump as he left the gravel path and continued across the well-worn dirt track to the clearing.

She wiped the tears from her cheeks, wishing she'd had the foresight to bring a compact or at least a tissue to repair the damage. Hopefully he wouldn't notice.

"I've been looking for you." Dylan stopped a few feet away, hands shoved in his pockets.

"It seemed more private here," Madison confessed, tucking her legs beneath her.

"If you want me to leave..."

"No." Madison stood, shaking the pine needles off her pants legs. "Please. I'd like the company."

It was quiet for a moment, then Dylan said, "Bob just checked out."

Madison nodded. "I expected as much."

"Look, Madison, I'm sorry I didn't believe you about your job."

"I didn't do much to inspire anyone's trust. Lying was a stupid thing to do, and now it's backfired right in my face."

"He had no right to fire you, though."

"Fire me?" Madison planted her hands on her hips, indignant at the thought. "Is that what he told you?"

Dylan stared at her, his brow furrowed. "He didn't fire you?"

"He most certainly did not!" Madison stomped a few feet down the path, itching to catch up with Bob and hurl some choice phrases right in his smug little face. "I quit!"

"You what?" He was almost slack-jawed with disbelief.

Madison turned back. "Someone who would steal my work and try to pass it off as his own is not someone I want to work for. Truth is, I've been unhappy at Donovan for a long time now. I just never had the guts to do anything about it."

"So what are you going to do now?" Dylan stepped close and brushed a strand of hair away from her face. She shivered at the contact.

"Look for a new job. It may take a while, though. I don't think I'll be getting good recommendations." She grimaced; as flip as she sounded, the thought still hurt.

A range of emotions played across his face. He looked thoughtful, angry, and finally concerned. "I guess the question now is, what do you *want* to do?"

The question danced in her head for a moment or two. It was an exciting sensation, being asked what she wanted. For as long as she could remember, she had done what was expected. Focus on her studies. Get good grades. Go into a practical field. Work her way up the ladder.

And when she chafed at the boundaries of family expectations and her own fears, the memory of her father's risk-taking and what it had cost him kept her in line.

Perhaps now she was ready to find a balance between what was expected and what she truly wanted.

"I have to go." A sense of urgency settled over her. It was time to take her life back from the fear that had permeated it for so long.

Dylan reached out and snagged her hand before she could take a step. "Wait. What's the hurry?"

She squeezed his hand, wishing she could cling forever to the warmth his touch created. "I have to get back to Seattle. I'd rather not drive after dark, so..."

"You're leaving tonight?" He sounded appalled at the prospect.

"I have to." To her horror, she could feel herself tearing up again. Summoning all her willpower, she forced back the tears.

"Stay one more night," he argued, his eyes pleading.

Madison closed her eyes, fighting to stand her ground. Her body was overwhelmed with the urge to sway towards him.

"I can't." She knew that if she stayed any longer, she would never be able to leave. And she knew she couldn't stay with the rest of her life in such turmoil.

Dylan stood quietly, a muscle working in his jaw. The pain she felt was echoed in his face.

With a soft cry, she threw her arms around him, pulling his head down for a kiss. It was full of sadness and desire and despair, and despite her best intentions the salt of her tears mingled with the sweetness of his mouth.

She breathed in his scent, a mix of soap and man and crisp ocean waves. Then she broke the kiss, backing away with one hand over her mouth.

"I'm so sorry, Dylan. Goodbye." And with one last, lingering glance over her shoulder, she ran down the path—and away from Westport.

Chapter Thirteen

"**A**re you okay, dear?"

"I'm fine."

"Maybe she'll come back."

Dylan handed his mom another pillowcase and walked to the window. It squeaked a little as he opened it; he made a mental note to take care of that next time he was doing maintenance chores around The Inn. "Madison's not coming back, Mom."

"But..."

"She was a very nice person and we went out a couple of times. So you can stop hovering like I'm about to collapse or something."

Ronnie dropped another pillow on the bed and turned to him, hands on her hips. "I'm not hovering. I'm just commenting. But you know how much I hate to interfere—" she ignored Dylan's snort "—so I won't say anything more on the subject."

"Good."

"But I do have one question." Waving away his mutinous

expression, she plowed ahead. "If you don't miss her, why are you here helping me clean out her cabin?"

Dylan grabbed the garbage bag and headed for the door. "Talk to you later, Mom," he tossed over his shoulder before escaping the room.

He'd never admit it to her, but his mother was right. With Carly still napping when he got home from fishing, he was at loose ends. An attempt at paperwork did little to clear his mind; neither did a jog on the beach. And his feet had carried him to what he now thought of as Madison's cabin before he even recognized where he was going.

It would have been okay if the cabin had been empty, but his mother caught sight of him lurking outside and, to forestall any uncomfortable questions, he pretended he'd dropped by to help her out.

That plan had been a miserable failure, too. She'd always been able to read him like a book.

Really, what had he been hoping to find by going to Madison's cabin? It was, as he suspected, sparkling clean even before his mother had gotten hold of it. A change of linens, fresh towels, newly-cut flowers, and it was ready for the next occupants.

No lingering trace of her scent in the air, no forgotten items, no evidence that Madison had stayed in that cabin at all, let alone for three weeks.

She was gone, and best forgotten. Her career, her friends, her life was in Seattle. He'd always known she was just passing through; it had been his own damn fault that he had allowed himself to start hoping for more. A relationship with a small-town single dad hadn't been enough to keep her here, and it wasn't enough to bring her back.

No matter how much he might want it to be.

Madison pulled another sadly neglected plant out of her box of belongings from Donovan, frowning over the limp greenery. Sighing, she placed it on the counter.

"They're all a bunch of idiots," Lily declared, lugging a box in from the car. "Don't waste another minute on Bob and his stupid cronies."

"I wasn't," Madison said, startled at the idea.

Lily eyed her critically. "I heard that sigh. Don't worry, you'll find another job."

"I don't care about the job."

"Hang on." Lily placed her hand on Madison's forehead. "No fever...should I check for a concussion?"

Madison slipped away from Lily and took her framed diploma out of the box. "Funny, Lil."

"I just don't know what's gotten into you. You've lived and breathed Donovan Development for years."

"Yeah, and look where it got me." She gestured around the room. "A boring, personality-free apartment, zero social life, and a box full of sad plants and paperwork. Believe me, I'm so glad I quit."

"Good for you," Lily said, patting her on the back. "So what's next?"

Madison shrugged. "Looking for a job, I guess. Although after my letter of resignation, I'm not counting on getting a good recommendation."

"You still haven't told me what was in that letter. All I know is the board looked downright stunned when they met to discuss it this afternoon."

Madison finished cleaning out the box and set it aside. "I just let them know exactly what Bob had done, as well as everything I'd put up with over the years. Lucky for me, I document well. Dates, times, places—it's all there. I thought they should know what kind of snake they have working for them."

Lily stared at her, goggle-eyed. "Who are you and what have you done with Madison?"

Madison laughed and rolled her eyes. "People do change, you know."

After an uncomfortable moment of scrutiny, Lily nodded slowly. "Sometimes they do. What changed you, Mad?"

Unbidden, an image of Dylan flashed through Madison's mind. She forced it down, but not before her fair skin gave her away.

Lily, of course, pounced. "A blush? There wouldn't be a man involved, would there?"

"Lily..."

"Did you catch a surfer like I told you to? Details, babe! I want to hear all about your torrid resort romance."

"Look, I'd rather not talk about it." Madison started in on her suitcase. In a daze since she'd returned to her empty apartment last night, she'd done little to settle back in other than retrieve her toothbrush.

"Ended badly, huh?" Lily's voice was laced with compassion.

"Hopefully, it hasn't ended at all," Madison said. "But I can't do anything about it until I get my job situation under control."

"So what are you going to do?"

"I know that I don't want another job like this one." Madison stacked neatly folded shirts in her dresser.

"Then what do you want?"

The question stopped her for a moment, carrying echoes of Dylan asking her the same thing. What did she want? Looking down, she saw the swimsuit Dylan had given her still tucked in the bottom of her suitcase.

What would it be like to really take a risk?

Suddenly, she knew what she wanted to do.

"Lily, what do you know about business licenses?" Ignoring the startled look on her best friend's face, she grabbed a pad and a pen. "Don't just stand there! I've got a lot to do in the next week. And I need your help."

And with a quick smile at Lily, Madison started to plan.

"Next item on our agenda is the purchase of flags for the downtown Fourth of July celebration. Mabel, will you give us your report?"

Dylan stifled a yawn as the council meeting stretched into its second hour. They'd covered old business and started in on the new, but the standing-room-only crowd was waiting for one topic—the resort-planning proposal from Donovan Development.

Bob Lee was sitting in the front row, shifting on his uncomfortable folding chair and not-so-surreptitiously checking his expensive watch every three minutes. His suit was impeccable; Dylan was pretty sure he could have sliced bread with the knife-edge creases in Bob's tailored slacks.

Stacked on the chair next to Bob were a laptop, a sheaf of handouts, and a flip chart. The man was definitely wandering into overkill territory.

Okay, he had a bit of a chip on his shoulder where Bob was concerned. Thanks to Mr. Donovan Development, Madison had disappeared from his life. And the more time that passed, the more he resented that fact.

"All those in favor, say 'aye'."

Dylan, startled from his wandering thoughts, mumbled his assent to the proposal. Thankfully, he had an agenda in front of him and had already decided to vote yes on the flag idea. He snuck a look at the clock on the far wall.

"We'll take a fifteen minute break before moving on to the next item," the council chairwoman announced, banging her gavel solemnly. The room immediately erupted into conversation, with chairs scraping back as people descended on the refreshments table.

Dylan rubbed the corded muscles at the back of his neck. The tension that had settled there seemed to be increasing. Maybe he should take a soak in the spa once this was over.

Stifling a sigh, he rose from his seat and moved over by the open window. A thin breeze curled through the screen, a welcome respite from the heat of the overcrowded room. He took a deep breath, letting the salt-tinged air fill his lungs and clear his mind.

Whatever personal issues he had with Donovan Development and its representative, Dylan had to be one hundred percent objective about the proposal. If it was the best thing for Westport, he would vote for it, no matter his opinion about the messenger.

The clink of metal on the glass water pitcher at the head table pulled Dylan's attention back to the room. Squaring his shoulders, he returned to his seat and looked out over the crowd that was now jostling back to the rows of seats.

The development proposal, the final item on tonight's agenda, was up next. Even now, Bob was rifling through his materials, preparing for his speech.

The view to the back of the room cleared as people sat, and Dylan let his gaze wander over the assembled crowd. He knew most of the people here; news had traveled fast about the potential development plan and the community had turned out in large numbers.

A row of people crowded along the back, leaning up against

the windowsills that lined the wall. Most were dressed in jeans and flannels, the official comfort wear of Westport. But one stood out from the rest, in a soft blue dress that draped over her curves like ocean waves hugging the shore.

Dylan blinked. That couldn't be...

The pounding gavel distracted him momentarily, and when he looked back she was gone. And he couldn't say if she had ever been there at all, or was just the product of a wistful—and vivid—imagination.

After a brief introduction, Bob stood to begin his presentation. The slide deck started with a video that combined artful shots of the ocean with artists' renderings of Donovan Development's vision for Westport. Multi-colored slides outlined cost-to-profit ratios, benefits to the community, and timelines in rapid succession. Even the flipchart was professionally done and artistic.

As Dylan listened to Bob's presentation, his heart sank. It was slick and professional, like the visual aids, and told the community exactly what they wanted to hear. But Dylan could sense the subtext. The flashy, high-profile resort would completely obliterate the small town feel of Westport.

Bob tied up his speech with a flourish and turned to the council member table. "I trust you will vote for the future of Westport, the future of each and every person in this room— Donovan Development's resort proposal."

"Thank you for your very illuminating presentation," the council chair said. "Before we take this proposal under consideration, we need to open the floor to comments and questions. Anyone?"

Several people rose from their seats and lined up at the microphone. Dylan took notes as they spoke out on the proposal, both pro and con. Public opinion appeared evenly divided. Those in favor spoke positively about the potential income boost for the economically depressed town; those against warned of the dramatic impact the fancy resort would have on the character of Westport.

Finally, the line of speakers dwindled to one. Dylan looked up as the last speaker took her place.

This time, there was no mistaking it. Madison was standing at the microphone, ready to speak.

Dylan sucked in a breath, stunned at the impact just the sight of her had on his system. His heart was beating a staccato against his chest. What was she doing here?

Unfortunately, Bob had the same thought. He leapt from his seat, face twisted in a mask of fury. "This woman has no right to speak," he yelled. His slightly nasal voice echoed in the hushed room. "She no longer works for Donovan and has no bearing on these proceedings."

Madison barely flinched. "If I may, I'd like the chance to speak."

"You're not a member of the community, and you're not here on official business," Bob sneered. "What possible reason could you have for being here?"

Dylan glanced out at the room. People were shifting in their seats, uncomfortable with the tone of the conversation.

Throughout it all, though, Madison remained calm. She stood quietly at the microphone, a sheaf of papers in her hands, waiting for Bob to finish.

When he sputtered to a halt, she spoke again. "I am not here as a representative of Donovan Development. However, I did sign up to speak at this meeting over two weeks ago, and I would like the opportunity to do so."

The secretary for the council checked her notes, shuffling papers until the right page was available. She nodded. "Her name is on the request, all right."

"But that was on behalf of Donovan Development," Bob protested.

"Nothing here says Donovan," the secretary said, pushing her glasses back up her nose. "Just Madison McIntyre."

The council chair stood. "I see no reason to deny Ms. McIntyre her chance to speak. Go ahead."

"Thank you." Madison looked at each of the council members in turn as she spoke, although Dylan noted that she shifted her gaze away from him quickly. "Four weeks ago I came to Westport under ... shall we say, less than honest pretenses. I was here to observe the community and develop a resort plan for my company, Donovan Development."

She glanced at Bob. "I no longer work for Donovan. But I can tell you that my resort plan, at the time I was an employee of the company, would have been quite similar to the one presented tonight."

The room was quiet as she spoke. "I also believe that this plan is a disservice to the community and completely wrong for Westport. Your town deserves better."

Bob leapt to his feet again. "Don't listen to her! She's just bitter because she was incompetent and had to resign. Our plan is exactly what Westport needs."

"Is it really?" Madison took the microphone from the stand, holding it in front of her as she spoke directly to her former boss. "Is it in Westport's interest to have three-quarters of the docks reserved for cruise ships and pleasure boats from out of town? Is it the best for the town that all the buildings on the waterfront be torn down and replaced with high-end boutiques? Do you think the people of Westport really want the beach approaches blocked off so vacationers staying in ten-story condos can enjoy the ocean by themselves?"

Dylan checked his notes. Sure enough, Bob's presentation

had glossed over the details, but Madison's description was true to what had been said.

"This plan may be what's best for Donovan Development, but I believe it is utterly wrong for Westport. The town has a unique character that shouldn't be pushed aside for another one of Donovan's ultra-chic resorts. That's why, on behalf of Coastal Development Services, I am here to present an alternative plan that preserves Westport's character while promoting sustainable tourism in the area."

By the end of her presentation, Madison had the gathered crowd eating out of her hand. In the interests of fair play, however, she stifled the ear-to-ear grin that threatened to take over and merely smiled politely at the city council's table.

"I have all the specifications right here." She waved a hand at the portfolio she'd leaned against the microphone stand before beginning her speech. "Would you like to take a look?"

"Your proposal sounds excellent," the council chair said, beckoning her forward. "Why don't you leave the paperwork with us and we'll look at both proposals more in-depth before making a final decision?"

"You can't do that!" Bob's strident voice broke in, startling Madison so much she almost dropped her papers. She'd almost forgotten he was even in the building. "If you even consider hiring this—this malcontent, I'll sue the town—and Madison!"

A red haze obscured Madison's vision for a moment. Then she turned, hands on hips, to confront him. "On what grounds?"

"Theft of intellectual property," he blustered. "Your proposal is based on research done while on Donovan's payroll."

"You kept all my research," she reminded him. "And there is nothing in my proposal that would be of the remotest interest to Donovan. Nothing extravagant, nothing high-powered—and the town receives the bulk of the tourist money. It's the exact opposite of everything Donovan stands for in resort development."

That shut him up, if only for a moment. Then his gaze swept over the city council before lighting on Dylan. "It wouldn't be a fair decision, anyway. Your lover is on the council. You've already slept your way to the contract."

Madison's gasp of outrage was drowned out by the scrape of Dylan's chair as he shoved to his feet. "I'd be careful what you say," he warned. "Madison would never do that, and you know it."

Bob sneered, "Oh, she wasn't good enough in bed to swing your vote, huh?"

"That's enough!" The council chair stood as well. "I won't have you maligning one of my council members or his friend. You're treading on very thin ice here, sir. And might I remind you that threatening lawsuits and casting slurs against a member of the council are not the best ways to support your proposal."

Chastened, Bob flushed and looked at the ground. "I sincerely apologize," he said, although Madison doubted he'd ever done anything sincerely in his life. "I was just concerned about the propriety of having the ... significant other of one of the presenters involved in the decision-making process."

Madison opened her mouth to protest that Dylan wasn't her significant other, but once again Dylan beat her to it. "The nature of my relationship with Ms. McIntyre will have no bearing on the decision, because I am withdrawing from the discussion. I trust the rest of the board to represent Westport well in this choice."

With that, he rounded the table and walked out of the room.

Everything that was in her urged Madison to follow, but she knew she had to present a professional image to the rest of the council. The rising voices of the gathered crowd quieted under the banging of the gavel. The council chair reminded everyone that the council would take into consideration both proposals as well as the feedback from the community. The final decision would be made by the end of the week.

Satisfied that she had done the best job possible, Madison handed her paperwork over to the council, along with a business card that listed her cell phone number and e-mail address. Silently thanking Lily for her help setting up Coastal Development on such short notice, she walked toward the door.

It took her longer than she had expected to leave; people stopped her progress every few steps to say hello or congratulate her on her presentation. She was surprised to realize just how many people she recognized from her short time living in Westport—and how many of them she would be proud to call her friends.

Finally, she reached her car and got in. A few deep breaths were necessary before she was calm enough to start the next part of her journey.

Because as nerve-wracking as her presentation before the city council had been, it was child's play compared to the pitch she had to make next.

Chapter Fourteen

He'd walked away.

It took everything in his power to move on out that door, when all he really wanted to do was grab Madison, drag her away with him, and ask her to stay with him forever.

Seeing her in the room tonight had made him realize just how much he'd missed her. He had been nearly overcome with fury when Bob had made those nasty comments about her, but Madison's calm composure throughout it all only reinforced what he knew about her.

She was strong, far stronger than he initially gave her credit for. And she was capable. Her professional presentation tonight had proven that.

And in a few short weeks in Westport, she had captured the essence of his hometown and built a vision for the future that honored it.

But her very professionalism had been the reason he had walked away.

He couldn't bear to jeopardize her future again.

She had a new job now, one that obviously suited her. If she got this contract—and he had little doubt that she would—she would be on the fast track to success.

And a single dad in a small town just couldn't compete with the draw of success on a bigger scale. In the long run, the lure of the city would pull her away. And this time, his heart wouldn't be able to take the loss.

Dylan cursed under his breath. Wasn't it just his luck that he would finally meet someone he could see spending his life with, and she was tied to the city as firmly as he was tied to Westport?

But there was no help for it now. She was on her way back to Seattle, and he was on his own.

Madison straightened her skirt and smoothed a lock of hair behind her ear. Taking a deep breath, she turned the knob and walked in the front door.

At this late hour, there was no one behind the desk. After a moment's hesitation, she tapped the bell for service.

"Can I help—" Dylan stopped in mid-sentence as he turned the corner from the family room. "Madison."

"Hi, Dylan." He looked even better than he had at the council meeting. Dark gray sweats topped by a fitted white t-shirt emphasized his muscular form. His hair was tousled, like he'd been running a hand through it.

She wanted to be the one running her hands through his hair.

"What are you doing here?" He looked wary; she hated the idea that she could have put that caution in his eyes.

She stuck a hand in her purse, rummaging for the piece of

paper. "I'm collecting on my silent auction bid," she said, placing the gift certificate on the counter between them.

He picked it up, a frown wrinkling his forehead. "You were the mystery bidder," he said. "But why?"

Madison shrugged, focusing on the countertop. "I knew I wanted to come back here. It seemed like a perfect opportunity."

Dylan pulled the reservation book towards him, running one long finger down the list of names. "You're even registered under 'certificate winner'."

She nodded. "I had Lily call in the reservation."

"And you did that because...?"

"I didn't want anyone to know I was going to be here before the meeting tonight," she said. "I needed the element of surprise so that I could catch Bob off-guard. Worked pretty well, don't you think?" She grinned at him, still heady with success.

"You were amazing," he said, slate-blue eyes locking with hers. A guarded intensity captured her gaze.

"Thank you," she whispered, throat dry as toast.

Dylan broke the connection first, glancing at the reservation book again. "Two nights, right?"

"At first."

He looked up sharply, brows drawn. "Then what?"

Madison took a deep breath. "Then we'll have to see what happens, won't we?"

Dylan sank into the heated water up to his shoulders. The spa was helping his body relax, but his mind wouldn't stop spinning at a hundred miles an hour.

Madison was here in Westport, staying at The Inn again.

But for how long? Was she here for the potential development contract, or more?

The sound of footsteps echoing off the path drew his attention. He turned in time to watch Madison step into the meadow, clothed only in a terry cloth robe.

"I thought I'd find you here," she said, nearing the hot tub. "Mind if I join you?"

Dylan shook his head mutely. Taking the gesture as an invitation, Madison tugged at the cord wrapped around her waist. It opened, and the robe slid from her shoulders.

Dylan was surrounded by water and steam, but his mouth was suddenly dry as the Gobi desert. She was wearing the bathing suit he'd given her.

It looked even more amazing than he remembered. Even in the filtered moonlight he could see the sparks of silver glinting off the midnight blue suit. It skimmed every curve, emphasizing her trim waist and lush breasts without being too revealing. She stepped up to the edge of the hot tub and dipped a toe in.

Madison let out a little sigh as she sank into the heated water. "Heavenly," she breathed.

Captivated by the shimmer of water droplets on her golden hair, Dylan was inclined to agree.

She stretched out on the stone bench, immersing herself in the bubbling water up to her neck. She closed her eyes, face tilted up to the sky.

Her foot bumped his. Dylan shifted in his seat, his body reacting immediately at the contact.

It was early yet. Any one of the other guests could drop by for a soak in the tub. Unfortunately.

He searched for a safe topic of conversation. "You seem to be enjoying your new job," he said finally.

Madison laughed, a soft chuckle that caught him right in the gut. "Immensely."

"Where is Coastal Development located, anyway?"

"Wherever I want it to be," she said.

His confusion must have shown on his face, because she laughed again and reached for his hand, lacing her fingers with his. "I *am* Coastal Development, Dylan. President, CEO, top employee and administrative assistant. I incorporated a few days ago."

"But why? You could have gotten a job with any company you wanted —why go out on a limb like that?"

Scooting closer, she leaned back against the edge of the hot tub and looked up at the star-filled sky. "To be honest, I really didn't enjoy working for Donovan. I just thought it was what I should do—work my way up someone else's ladder, create projects that met their vision, follow the party line. So when my job evaporated, I decided to take a risk."

Her hair softly brushed his shoulder as she turned. "More than one risk, to tell you the truth." Eyes drifting shut, she leaned forward and touched her lips feather-light to his.

The temperature in the hot tub shot up several degrees as she slid one water-slicked hand up his arm to tangle in his dampened hair. Dylan groaned deep in his throat and wrapped his arms around her, hauling her forward until she was settled in his lap. He tilted his head just a fraction, enough to deepen the kiss.

The tips of her breasts, taut and beaded underneath the slick fabric of the bathing suit, brushed against his heated chest. Water lapped between them as he slid his hands down her back to grip her hips, pulling her closer.

She moaned against his lips and stroked her hands down his back, caressing the play of muscles as the water gently lifted them in a rocking motion.

Dylan trailed his hand from her hip up her side, reveling in the shiver that traveled through her entire body at the touch.

He pulled back from her kiss long enough to whisper hoarsely, "God, you are so beautiful." Then his mouth descended on hers, his hand stroking the soft, damp curve of her waist.

This time, Madison broke the kiss, throwing her head back until her hair trailed in the steaming water. Her breath came in little pants as Dylan planted kisses down her neck. Then he pulled back and looked at her.

Madison's water-drenched skin shone in the filtered moonlight, her golden hair trailing in the water like a mermaid. Her mouth was slightly open, her eyes closed. She was his every fantasy, his every wish for the future come true, and she was in his arms.

Then her eyes opened and she moved, pushing on his shoulders until he was pressed back against the edge of the tub. She straddled him, her thighs around his waist, pressing against his straining erection.

"Madison," he said, though he wasn't sure if it was a warning or a plea.

Her hand trailed down his chest, past his abs, and delved beneath the waistband of his swimsuit. And then, oh God, she was stroking him, making his hips buck beneath her.

"You have to stop," he hissed, holding on to the last shreds of his self-control.

"No I don't," she crooned, rubbing her thumb over the broad tip of his cock.

"But I'm going to—" He clamped his mouth shut as she moved off him, silently urging him up until he was seated on the smooth river stones at the edge of the hot tub.

She moved between his legs, which dangled in the steamy water, and tugged at the waistband of his board shorts. Breath hissed out between his teeth as his cock sprang free, hard and straining against his stomach.

With a soft smile, she leaned forward and took him in her mouth.

A shudder ran through him as she stroked him with her tongue, damp heat surrounding him. Her blond hair spread out on the surface of the water, tangling in the currents. She looked like a mermaid, One hand cupped his sac, squeezing lightly.

With a groan, he threaded his fingers through her hair and held on, thrusting into her avid mouth as he gave himself up to the exquisite pleasure. She swirled her tongue around the sensitive tip, then dove deep again, setting up a rhythm that sucked him deep into the maelstrom.

The sound of the surf roared in his ears as she took him higher and higher until the wave crested and he exploded deep in her mouth. Collapsing on the patio surrounding the hot tub, propped up by his elbows, he struggled to catch his breath.

Madison boosted herself out of the hot tub, steam rising off her slick body as the cool of the night air met her water-heated skin. She leaned over and kissed him, then collapsed right next to him.

Dylan tucked himself back in his shorts and let out a long, shaky sigh. "I can't believe you did that," he said.

"Do you mind?" A quick glance at her face showed that she was only half kidding. Sometimes he had to remind himself that she wasn't as experienced as he expected her to be.

"Mind? Are you kidding?" He rolled to the side and pulled her head down for a kiss. "That was amazing."

She blushed.

"But we can't stay."

Her face showed her confusion. "Why not?"

"Because this is a public hot tub, and I have a feeling we may have visitors soon."

Her blush went from a delicate pink to fire-engine red in moments. "Oh, my goodness! I completely forgot."

"I know." He grinned at her, then stretched an arm behind him and snagged the towels. "So did I, for a moment. But now is a different story."

"Who'd have thought that you'd be the practical one," she laughed, swiping her towel down both arms.

Dylan stood and held out a hand, helping her up. "I'll have you know that I'm extremely practical."

"Good." She grabbed her robe and slipped it on. "So why don't you show me the quickest way back to the cabins. That seems practical, doesn't it?"

"Absolutely," he said, grabbing her hand and pulling her down the path behind him.

They were both giggling and out of breath when Dylan shut the door to her cabin behind them.

The slight weight of embarrassment following her uncharacteristic sexual aggressiveness had lifted with the ease of their laughter. She felt comfortable with Dylan. Comfortable in her own skin.

Which she wanted to feel next to Dylan's skin as soon as possible.

She sucked in a breath as another wave of desire rushed through her. She'd never experienced desire on this level before meeting Dylan. But it was a constant state for her when she was around him.

As if he could read her thoughts, he turned to her, the laughter in his eyes fading as it was overtaken with heat. "Come here," he murmured.

She went willingly. Lips touched, tongues tangled, as a gentle kiss quickly turned passionate. Then he picked her up and carried her over to the neatly made bed.

"It's too tidy in here," he said, pulling back the covers and setting her down. "I think it's time to muss things up a bit."

"I like that idea." Madison wrapped her arms around his neck and pulled him down on top of her. "I like it a lot."

They moved quickly to remove their swimsuits, tossing them on the floor by the bed. Then Madison rolled over so she was within reach of the nightstand and opened the drawer. She pulled out a handful of square packets.

Dylan raised an eyebrow. "Confident?"

"Hopeful." She reached for him, but he moved out of the way.

"Lie down." He waited until she complied, then stretched out next to her. He stroked her with one strong, calloused hand, sensitizing every inch of her body until she was quivering beneath his touch. Then, and only then, did he touch her where she ached for it.

She was already wet and ready for him. He slid his finger in and out, over and over, until her hips lifted with each motion. Rolling away, he grabbed a packet and ripped it open, smoothing the condom over his waiting erection in record time.

Then he settled between her open legs and slowly pressed inside her.

Madison groaned as he filled her, stretching muscles long unused. Warmth radiated out from her core as he thrust into her again and again.

She lifted her legs and wrapped them around his waist, holding on as his movement took on a faster pace. He slid in and out, like waves rolling onto the shore, and she abandoned herself to the exquisite sensation.

Faster and faster they moved, bodies slick with sweat, until her release crashed over her, sweeping her along on waves of passion. Moments later he followed, collapsing on her with a hoarse shout.

Long minutes passed as they lay together, hearts pounding, breath panting. Finally he rolled to the side, still holding her, though she missed the heady sensation of his weight on her.

He stroked her hair, watching her face with a penetrating gaze. "Penny for your thoughts," he said at last.

"Wow," she said, since it was all she could come up with at the moment.

He laughed. "Hold that thought." He slid off the bed, as graceful as a cat, and padded into the bathroom. Moments later he returned, holding a warm washcloth.

When she was done, he took it back to the bathroom and then came back to the bed, sliding in next to her and pulling the covers up over them both.

"So you were saying?" He bent his elbow and propped his head on his palm.

She burst out laughing. "I believe the word was 'wow'."

"Good. Wanted to make sure I had that right."

"Oh, you definitely did." She was quiet for a moment. "Thank you."

His brows drew together. "What for?"

"An amazing night," she stammered, confused at the sudden change in his demeanor.

"It wasn't a favor, Madison. No thanks needed." He looked away. "So, how soon do you have to be back in Seattle?"

She shook her head. "I don't intend to go back to Seattle at all, except to visit."

"So you're..."

"Moving to Westport," she completed for him. "Permanently, I hope."

"You're kidding."

"Dylan, I named the company Coastal Development for a reason. I want to create sustainable, low-key coastal development, so what better place to work?"

"What if you don't get this contract?"

"I will," she said with confidence, then sat quietly for a moment. "But even if I don't, I have another reason for moving here."

"Which is?"

"I love you," she said, gripping his hand tightly. "And this is a risk I'm willing to take."

"Is it still a risk if I love you back?" He brushed damp tendrils of hair back from her forehead.

"If it is, I'm looking forward to being a risk taker on a regular basis."

If anyone had been walking past the cabin right then, they would have been startled by the burst of laughter that floated out to the star-filled sky.

Epilogue

Dylan was mooring the boat up at the dock when the sound of footsteps caught his attention. Slim, toned legs, topped by khaki shorts, sauntered into his field of vision.

He stood, hands on hips, and gave Madison a slow, ankles-to-hairline ogle. Her fair skin blushed prettily under his appreciative gaze.

"Hey, sailor," she called, coming to a halt in front of *The Lucky Strike*. "Can I buy you a drink?"

Dylan pushed his baseball cap back and swiped his forehead. The day was already unseasonably warm, but being around Madison tended to raise his body temperature even more. "Sounds great," he said. Turning to the charter boat, he called down into the galley, "John, I'm taking off. You got those papers signed yet?"

A disembodied hand, clutching a sheaf of legal-looking papers, shot up through the open stairwell. "Here you go," John's voice echoed from below.

Dylan reached over, plucked the papers from John's hand,

and tucked them in his back pocket. Turning to Madison, he held out his hand and linked his fingers with hers. "Come on, let's get out of here," he said, pulling her up the ramp behind him.

By unspoken agreement, they walked into the Seafood Shack and took the last booth in the back corner. Dylan hailed Sallie and requested two large colas as they sat.

"I have some news," Madison said, barely containing a grin.

"You got the contract!" Dylan leaned over the table and planted a kiss on her. "Congratulations!"

Madison pushed her lower lip out in a mock pout. "Who told?"

He tucked a strand of hair behind her ear, caressing her cheek. "You did—your face gave you away. Besides, Westport would have to be crazy to pick a Donovan project over yours."

"Lucky for me, the city council is highly intelligent."

"I've always thought so."

Sallie brought over the colas and slid them onto the table, shaking her head at their linked hands. "Watch the PDA's, you two," she warned. "This is a family establishment." With a wink, she returned to the counter.

"But that's not the only news," she said, smiling wickedly at him.

"Okay, I'll bite. What's up?"

"I heard from Donovan Development today. Seems Bob is no longer in their employ."

Dylan grinned at her. "Lost the contract and the job in one fell swoop, huh?"

"I think my letter of resignation had something to do with it, too. In any case, they've asked me to come back to work. Even threw in a promotion, a raise, and creative autonomy over this project."

Dylan's heart stuttered. Summoning up an encouraging smile, he said, "So what are you going to do?"

Madison grinned at him. "Are you kidding? They couldn't pay me enough."

Dylan sighed with relief and took a swig of his cola.

"Dylan, I'm not going anywhere," Madison said, caressing his hand.

He leaned forward and gave her a quick kiss. "I know."

"So what were you talking with John about?" Madison took a long sip of her cola, tilting her head to get a glimpse of the papers stuffed in Dylan's jeans pocket.

"Just some legal stuff, working out details of his promotion."

"Promotion?" Madison glanced quizzically at Dylan. "What are you talking about?"

Shifting, Dylan retrieved the papers and placed them in the center of the table. "As of next Monday, John is the new captain of *The Lucky Strike.*"

"He is? But how? Why?"

Dylan shrugged. "Time for a change. He's more than ready for it."

Madison gripped his hands tightly. "Dylan, if you're doing this because of me, don't. I'm fine with you being a charter-boat captain. I don't want you to give up something important just because I freaked out about it once."

"Good, because I have no intention of giving it up permanently." He leaned over and kissed her cheek. "I'm still the owner of Oceanic Charters, and I'll be John's replacement skipper when he needs a day off. But to be honest, I've been ready to focus my attention on other things for a while now. You just inspired me to go after what I really want."

Madison blushed again, turning her fair skin an attractive shade of pink. "And what do you really want?"

His thumb traced lazy patterns on the back of her hand. "I

want to spend more time on my web design business. I turn down way too many jobs in the fishing season, and I think my business will really take off if I don't limit the months I work on it."

"Sounds reasonable," she said.

"Thanks. Don't interrupt," he teased. "Second, I want a house. I'll be forever grateful to Mom for helping out with Carly, but it's time for us to be a family on our own."

Dylan cleared his throat. "In fact, I found a perfect house for sale yesterday. Why don't you come take a look at it with me?"

Madison nodded and they stood to leave. Dylan dropped a few bills on the table to cover the cost of their drinks, and they walked out into the sunlight.

A few minutes in the car and they were pulling up in front of a tidy two-story home on a large lot, just a block from the ocean. Dylan unlocked the front door and ushered Madison inside.

"Oh, Dylan, it's perfect," she breathed, turning in a slow circle in the empty living room. The hardwood floors shone under her feet, and a fireplace beckoned from the far wall. She walked towards it, frowning at the envelope propped on the mantel. "It looks like the owner forgot something," she said, picking it up.

"Take a closer look," he said, wandering nonchalantly to the window. He glanced surreptitiously at her.

"This has my name on it... what on earth?" She opened the envelope and read the note inside aloud. "'Perfect for snuggling in front of a roaring fire on a cold winter night.' Dylan?"

"Let's look around." Avoiding the question in her eyes, he swept a hand in front of him, mutely encouraging her to lead the way.

In the kitchen, another envelope waited atop the stove. "'Hot meals around a family table.'"

She frowned quizzically at him as she tried the family room next. "'Relaxing after a day at the beach.'"

Upstairs, she tried the first bedroom, Dylan following closely behind. "'Tucking Carly into bed.' Dylan, what –"

"Just keep looking," he reassured.

The room across the hall was the master bedroom. The expected envelope was resting on the sill of the large picture window, overlooking the fenced backyard. The ocean could be seen over the treetops. "'Waking up in your arms.'"

"Try this door," Dylan urged. She slipped past him, her eyes suspiciously bright.

This envelope was on a window seat just waiting for plump cushions. She opened the envelope. "'A perfect home office.'" This time, another piece of paper slipped out of the envelope with the note and fluttered to the floor. She picked it up with hands that shook just a little. It was a business card, imprinted with the slogan, "Coastal Development and Web Design. Dylan and Madison Edwards, owners."

Madison looked up, eyes wide, and gasped.

Dylan held out a black velvet box, lid opened to reveal the glittering ring inside. "Will you make these dreams come true?"

With a soft cry, she flung her arms around him. "Of course," she said, laughing and crying at the same time.

He slipped the ring on her finger and kissed her gently. And there, in the empty house they would fill with love and laughter, they celebrated the risk that, in the end, was no risk at all.

Acknowledgments

This book is my love letter to the Washington coast – and I hope you enjoyed reading it as much as I enjoyed writing it!

First thanks go to my husband, who grew up on the coast and introduced me to the region. He's a wealth of information about the coast, from the history to the geography to the weather patterns, and I couldn't have written this without his input.

Second, I appreciate all those who worked (or work) in the charter fishing industry who entertained my questions and shared great info on it. Special thanks go to my brother-in-law, John, who spend a few summers on a charter boat as a teen.

Thanks to my amazing author friends, for the support, encouragement, cheerleading, wine, and tapas. Looking forward to spending time with you in person soon. Rachel, Serena and Kris, I wouldn't have jumped into indie publishing without your support – thank you so much! And thanks also to Maia, my first and most awesome beta reader and critique partner.

Hugs and gratitude to my wonderful kids. You all rock.

And big thanks to you, the readers. I appreciate you sticking with me through the years!

About the Author

From food to fiction, Kate likes things spicy! Award-winning, bestselling contemporary romance author Kate Davies writes books featuring strong, sexy men and women finding their happily ever afters. She enjoys traveling, reading, trying new recipes, and spending time with family and friends. Kate lives in the Pacific Northwest with her husband.

Also by Kate Davies

Seattle Nights

Taking the Cake

Strip Tease

Challenging Carter

Girls Most Likely To...

Most Likely To Succeed

Cutest Couple

Life of the Party

Royals and Rebels

Lessons in Love

Lessons in Trust

Pour Decisions

No Way, Rosé

Standalone

Hallowed Love

Home for Christmas

Going for Broke